# THE ORGANIC CHURCH

*For Virginia,
I love you in
the Lord,
Clay Watts*

# THE ORGANIC CHURCH

A Story of Revival

Clay Watts

Copyright © 2017 Clay Watts
All rights reserved
Cover design © 2017 by Ben Watts
Edited by Dr. Kathy Watts and Lori Janke

ISBN-13: 9781545255384
ISBN-10: 1545255385
Library of Congress Control Number: 2017905658
CreateSpace Independent Publishing Platform
North Charleston, South Carolina

No portion of this work may be reproduced in any fashion except by express permission in writing from the author.

*Dedicated to leaders in the church who know there is more – and want to see it happen.*

# Table of Contents

Introduction · · · · · · · · · · · · · · · · · · · · · · · · · · · · · · · · · · · ix

1  Good News and Bad News · · · · · · · · · · · · · · · · · · · · · · · ·1
2  Church Busyness · · · · · · · · · · · · · · · · · · · · · · · · · · · · · ·5
3  The Family Vacation · · · · · · · · · · · · · · · · · · · · · · · · · · · 13
4  The Sabbatical Begins · · · · · · · · · · · · · · · · · · · · · · · · · 18
5  Mark and Breakthrough · · · · · · · · · · · · · · · · · · · · · · · · 26
6  Going Deeper · · · · · · · · · · · · · · · · · · · · · · · · · · · · · · · 37
7  Gabe and the Oberlins · · · · · · · · · · · · · · · · · · · · · · · · 42
8  George and Bob · · · · · · · · · · · · · · · · · · · · · · · · · · · · · 47
9  Preparation · · · · · · · · · · · · · · · · · · · · · · · · · · · · · · · · 57
10 Back Home · · · · · · · · · · · · · · · · · · · · · · · · · · · · · · · · 64
11 Back in the Office · · · · · · · · · · · · · · · · · · · · · · · · · · · 68
12 The Family Budget · · · · · · · · · · · · · · · · · · · · · · · · · · 73
13 The Men's Group and Retreat · · · · · · · · · · · · · · · · · 80
14 The T-shirt Incident · · · · · · · · · · · · · · · · · · · · · · · · · 90
15 The Organic Church Revealed · · · · · · · · · · · · · · · · · 95
16 The Organic Church Made Real · · · · · · · · · · · · · · · 108
17 The End Times Teacher · · · · · · · · · · · · · · · · · · · · · 113
18 This Is It! · · · · · · · · · · · · · · · · · · · · · · · · · · · · · · · · 120
19 Next Steps · · · · · · · · · · · · · · · · · · · · · · · · · · · · · · · 123
20 Evaluating the Outpouring · · · · · · · · · · · · · · · · · · · 130
21 The Seminars · · · · · · · · · · · · · · · · · · · · · · · · · · · · 134

| 22 | Family Tensions | 138 |
| 23 | The Family Sabbatical | 143 |
| 24 | The First Year and Beyond | 145 |
| | Epilogue | 159 |
| | About the Author | 163 |

# Introduction

Jerry Smith is the lead pastor of a growing, spirit-filled church. He has devoted his life to building a ministry, shepherding his people, and providing for his family. This is a story of how he learns, in unexpected ways, to desire, prepare for, and steward a revival. While the characters and incidents are purely fictional, the story has come out of experiences my wife and I have had over many years in a variety of churches, large and small, denominational and non-denominational.

Most recently, we have taught Restoring Relationships classes for hundreds of people at two churches, one very large and one very small. The program was founded by Christian psychologist Dominic Herbst, and we have seen it help mature believers recognize and get freedom from intentional and unintentional past hurts that thwart God's purpose for them. I believe this is a key element of preparing for revival, along with several others that are illustrated in Jerry's story. He wants to lead his church into greater levels of intimacy with God, but he encounters real world distractions and obstacles. As he overcomes them through persistence and determination, he discovers unimagined insight into how the church can prepare for the revival that is surely coming before Christ returns for His spotless Bride.

# 1

## Good News and Bad News

Pastor Jerry Smith was about to unlock his front door when it flew open. A sandy-haired, blue-eyed boy grinned and said excitedly, "You're home for dinner! We're having catfish. How was your day?"

With a smile on his face, he hugged his son, Steve, and lifted him off the ground. "Fried? With red sauce? Yum! My day was great and is about to get even better. How was yours?"

"Not bad. My teacher really liked my project on New Zealand. She said it was creative and fun. I got a 95!"

"Good job. I'm proud of you, son!" Jerry thought how far this ten-year-old had come in the five years since his diagnosis of severe dyslexia. "You put a lot of work into that project. Congratulations."

As Jerry dropped his backpack in the study, his other son and daughter greeted him from the family room with a couple of "Hi, dads." His wife, Donna, gave him a big "Hi, honey," and said, "Dinner in about 15 minutes, if that's ok." Jerry kissed her and said, "You bet. I'll go change."

Around the dinner table, between the catfish, coleslaw, and hushpuppies, the conversation rambled from schoolwork and sports to the latest happenings at the church. Stephanie asked how many other youth were signed up for the Brazil missions trip and who they were. Don wanted to talk about the junior high ski trip coming up over spring break. Finally, Jerry broke in and said, "I've got a surprise for all of you." After the chatter quickly ceased, he continued. "The church board met last night, and they have given me a sabbatical this summer, right after the missions trip. It's for a month, and they took up an offering so we can have a family vacation for two weeks of that. Where should we go?"

Steve was first with a loud, "New Zealand! It will be wonderful!" Donna beamed at Jerry while the others chimed in with their suggestions. Jerry had already called her with the news, and she had asked him to involve the children in the decision. It was fun to see their enthusiasm and creativity as Stephanie and Don countered Steve with equally exotic destinations. Finally, Donna suggested, "Why don't we all pray and ask God's guidance? I'm sure He'll speak to each of us and we can make a decision in the next few days." Steve was pretty sure that God loved New Zealand, so he quickly agreed and offered to start off the prayer.

After each family member prayed in turn, they quietly went about their evening studies and chores, thinking about what a wonderful opportunity this would be for their family. Donna also prayed that the church would be blessed through the gift her husband would have of a two-week sabbatical. God knew, she thought, that he was under a lot of pressure, and this was the perfect answer to her prayers for him and the family.

Since finding out earlier in the day, Jerry had been contemplating how he would use the sabbatical time. He was happy to leave the vacation decision and planning to Donna and the kids, knowing that he would finally have a time to rest and recharge. The latest building program had been draining, and several staff and volunteer leader changes had left his portfolio larger than it had been in years. He was now the leader of the hospitality team, as well as the men's group and the new member program. And, oh yes, the main preacher for Sunday mornings and Wednesday evenings. He was in the middle of helping the Oberlins find a part-time nursery director, and he was also about to launch a new men's discipleship program that would culminate in an annual retreat with special speakers and activities. It involved training several volunteer coaches who would then be responsible for groups of men throughout the year. Jerry was committed to leading this effort personally, but it was taking more time than he had thought.

Yes, he could certainly use a sabbatical. He had been running full speed for so many years now, and he needed an opportunity to stop and get his bearings. He decided that, just as his family prayed about the vacation opportunity, he would pray about his sabbatical period. In an uncharacteristic burst of inspiration, he determined to enlist his wife, his associate pastor, Mark Henson, and a longtime friend, George James, to pray with him about how best to plan for and use the two weeks.

The next day, Jerry found himself back in the middle of typical church issues. He hardly had time to enlist his prayer team, much less begin to pray about the summer sabbatical himself. His first minor crisis was the nursery director opening. Mary Oberlin, the children's pastor, wanted to upgrade the open position so she could eventually offer a day care program during the week. Many of the staff and young couples had been asking about such a program, so she decided to use the opening to discuss her ideas with Jerry. Jerry was not looking forward to the discussion. He was concerned that expansion to a full day care could be an administrative distraction and place heavier demands on the building and maintenance staff. Jerry wanted to hear what Mary had to say, but he was not going to be persuaded easily.

Mary and her husband Tom, the youth pastor, had thought through the position upgrade and made a strong case for transitioning to a day care facility. Jerry thanked them and promised to pray about it. Just as he was going to call his wife to brief her on their proposal, Mark Henson, the associate pastor, rushed into his office and announced, "Pastor, come quickly. You gotta see this!" Jerry followed Mark to the back parking lot where they saw a tree-trimming crew working on the huge oak tree that framed the parking lot entrance. A power line ran across the back of the property, and over the years the upper branches of the tree had grown above and below the line. The crew had already taken down several large limbs, and it was clear that the shape of the beautiful old tree was being destroyed forever.

Jerry, followed by Mark, rushed across the asphalt lot, picked out the crew supervisor, and began to demand that he stop butchering the tree. The supervisor politely interrupted and apologized about having to trim the tree, but made it clear that the utility easement provides for tree maintenance. He assured them that the tree is being "re-shaped" according to company standards that were approved many years ago by the state utility commission. Jerry wrote down the man's name from his ID badge and asked who else they could speak to. The supervisor handed him the company's standard brochure and pointed to the customer service hotline. Jerry started to yell, "Are you kidding me?" but could only get out a sputtering gasp of unbelief. Mark detected an imminent disaster, pulled Jerry aside, and said, "Pastor, it's too late, the damage is done. Anyway, you know we are not going to prevail with the utility company. Let's not let this get to us." Jerry reluctantly agreed, but could not talk all the way back to his office.

Finally, with his door closed to his office, he not so silently complained to God. "How could You let this happen? Our trees are admired by everyone. After all the money we spent on the new building and landscaping to make this place beautiful, this is a slap in the face!" Then, after realizing what he almost had said to the crew supervisor, he finally admitted under his breath, "OK, Lord, I let this get to me. There is too much going on. I really need that sabbatical!"

After Jerry composed himself, he decided that, while the idea of a day care had a lot of merit, the time was not right to commit to something that substantial. Perhaps they could offer a smaller version of a once or twice a week morning mother's day out. This would meet some of the needs of the staff and congregation, justify a position upgrade, and determine the administrative impact of the additional facilities and staff utilization. Not a bad compromise. When Jerry presented this solution to the Oberlins, they quickly agreed to modify their position description and start looking for the director position as soon as the church board approved the upgrade.

The rest of the day was full of interruptions and fire-fighting. Jerry had to work late, so the family summer vacation discussion was unintentionally postponed. Donna and the kids grabbed a quick bite and spent the evening on homework. When Jerry returned to the peace and quiet of his home, he realized the contrast with his hectic day and thought that he really needed to spend more time with Donna and the kids.

# 2

## Church Busyness

After seeing the damage done to the oak tree the following day, and trying not to rekindle his anger over an iced coffee while waiting for his lunch order, Jerry's mind wandered to the nursery and pre-school position decision. He congratulated himself on avoiding an administrative hassle, however, he had an uneasy feeling about how it was done. Was it another logical, well thought out process without a lot of prayer and listening to the Holy Spirit? Or did they really find God's will in the matter? He hadn't specifically prayed with the Oberlins, and they didn't mention to him that they had taken time to pray. He assumed they had, of course, but it was a bit disturbing that no one, especially he, had thought of praying as a group about this important decision. Even more disturbing was that they did not really seek the Lord about the position description. It was an old one that was edited briefly to indicate the slightly increased responsibilities and qualifications. But no one thought to see if there were other items that should be considered. Should there be a clear, practical objective about having a positive impact on the spiritual, emotional, and physical health of these young children? Many of them have no other opportunity for godly men and women to speak into their little lives and create a rich atmosphere of love and worship. As Jerry began to think about some of the pre-schoolers he knew, he was sorry for his casual attitude toward this neglected part of the ministry. He inwardly committed to discussing this with the Oberlins and to spend quality time with them in prayer to see what God wanted them to do with His precious ones. Perhaps they had already prayed over these issues, but he wanted to make sure he was a part of it.

On his way back to the church, Jerry began to think about the other ministries in the church. Was he involved enough in them? Had he spent time in prayer with the leaders over each one to see what changes God might have in store for them? Should he just trust that the leaders were already doing that? What was his role, anyway? The more he thought about it, the more concerned he became. When he sat down at his desk, he took a deep breath, said a quick prayer, and forced himself to write these questions in his journal. Seeing them in black and white relieved some of the stress he was starting to feel. He then committed to pray about what he should do generally, and specifically, in each area. He knew that the upcoming sabbatical was not an accident. He felt like he was to use the time to really hear from God about his involvement in key areas of the church. He felt that he needed to be, if not in control, at least intimately aware of what was going on in each area.

The next week, as he was beginning to prepare for Sunday's sermon, Jerry had the distinct impression that there was one more task for his time away. It was the most important of all. He heard the phrase, "Prepare for revival." The word "revival" struck fear and awe in Jerry's heart. He had been down this road several times with scheduled week or two week long "revival" meetings conducted by an outside evangelist holding nightly services. Each time his optimism and faith were rewarded with what looked like feeble results, or no results at all. He had seen other churches fare even worse when a longer term revival turned sour because of financial or moral misconduct of one of the leaders.

He had finally come to the conclusion that there was no point in trying to make a revival happen. He had to admit to God that deep in his heart he had given up on seeing a significant outward and community-impacting move of the Holy Spirit in his ministry. Nevertheless, he felt that between now and the beginning of his sabbatical, he needed to study past revivals. It would provide good sermon material in any event. He even held a glimmer of hope that he might uncover some pointers that would prepare the way for, if not a major revival, at least a renewal and rededication of his staff, his congregation, and himself, to know God more intimately. Jerry had learned that he could do a topical study over several months only if he scheduled time every week to work on it. So he blocked out Tuesday mornings to pray about his agenda for the sabbatical month and to read and journal about past revivals.

Over the next few months leading up to the family vacation and his time away, Jerry's life was packed with sermon preparation, church activities, staff issues, and church members needing his personal attention. He had begun to do some reading about revivals, but quickly realized that much of what he wanted to cover was going to have to wait. He continued to use part of Tuesday mornings to pray that his heart would be ready to hear from God during his time away, but there was no way he could spend quality time on research and still meet all of his regular church and family responsibilities.

An example was the worship leader incident. Gabe Miller was the young and talented worship leader with a musical wife and toddler daughter. He had been introducing new worship songs that stretched some of the long-time members. A couple of them brought their concerns to Pastor Jerry. He reluctantly agreed to meet with them to hear what their issues were. After listening to them, he scheduled a meeting with Gabe to discuss what the issues were with the new songs. Gabe said that he was puzzled. The songs were from a new album by a well-known worship artist and band. They had already been used by many churches, and Gabe had only heard glowing reports from other worship leaders.

As Jerry and Gabe together reviewed the tracks and the lyrics in detail, Jerry saw that the themes and words were not as scripturally based as most of the songs in the main worship services. Gabe explained that many younger people did not seem engaged in the worship time, and he was trying to find music with lyrics that would be more meaningful to them while still supporting the preaching topics. Jerry knew he had to be careful in critiquing Gabe. He did not want to be in the position of approving or vetoing Gabe's song selections. Their understanding had been that he would discuss with Gabe his sermon topics and the themes he wanted to emphasize, and Gabe would choose a song list that would complement that and create a strong atmosphere of worship and praise. Gabe had always done an excellent job of praying and seeking the Holy Spirit's guidance, and Jerry did not want to inhibit Gabe's musical and spiritual gifts. Nevertheless, he felt that it was his role as the senior pastor to set the guidelines and tone of the main services.

When he suggested to Gabe that the words were just as important, if not more so, than the music, he was not expecting the reaction he got. Gabe was offended. His offense wasn't so much because of the specifics of the songs, but because he felt that Jerry didn't trust his ability to prayerfully select the right songs. He was not angry with Jerry, just hurt. Gabe agreed, however, to listen and take Jerry's ideas as constructive advice. Jerry proceeded to give examples of how lyrics can lead people into God's presence to receive encouragement, direction, and healing. Even more importantly, thoughtful lyrics can help people draw nearer to Him. Gabe agreed and offered other examples of meaningful song lyrics, and then began to see that every precious moment in a worship service either leads people towards God, or allows them to lose their focus with well-intentioned, but general sentiments.

As the conversation wound down, Jerry felt that Gabe finally had a clearer understanding of the purpose of worship music and the characteristics of lyrics that would have the greatest impact on the congregation. When Gabe left, Jerry realized that, once again, he desperately needed to use the sabbatical time to sit back and take stock of every area of the ministry. In just a few minutes, by "staying in the ring" even when it was uncomfortable, he was able to convince Gabe of a critical aspect of the ministry. He was determined to be more proactive in recognizing and dealing with potential lack of focus throughout the ministry, especially where he could clarify goals and direction as the senior pastor.

Later in the week, Jerry began to see that the song lyrics incident and the nursery leader situation were examples not just of keeping the staff moving in the same direction, but even more importantly, they underscored the need for him to be very sure about the overall mission and objectives of the church. The more he prayed about this heavy responsibility, the more he realized that he needed to be in agreement with God's purpose for the church. He concluded that depended completely on his personal relationship with the Lord. Was he getting distracted with attractive but ultimately unproductive activities? He believed he had avoided such a potential distraction by not expanding the nursery program to include weekday care. But was that really true? Was he missing the Holy Spirit's intent to focus on the Word and to make it personally relevant to his congregation? What was he really supposed to be focusing on, anyway?

And after all of his best intentions to pray about important items like these, he could not even remember if he prayed with Gabe about that incident. Why was he unable to do the things he knew he should be doing? Only a deep and unhindered relationship with God could possibly give him the answers to these critical questions. And only then could he see the transformation in people's hearts and behavior for which he so desperately longed. That's what was missing – a real change in the hearts and minds of his congregation and the community they serve. He realized that this kind of change could only come about if he were completely yielded to God in his own life.

As if the devil were listening in on Jerry's thoughts, the next day he began to be bombarded with situation after situation that challenged everything he stood for and wanted to achieve. First, Donna complained about lack of progress on the vacation plans. Jerry had not called a family meeting on this since Donna first asked everyone to pray about it two weeks ago. The children would mention it from time to time, but they were all over the place on what they wanted to do. She was not able to bring any of them to agreement on a common solution. Her vision for a nice family getaway was completely different from any of theirs. She told Jerry that he had to take the lead on this matter – she was not able to handle it.

Then Mark, his associate pastor, came to him with a dilemma regarding the small groups. One of the leaders suggested that adhering to the standard curriculum was often stifling their group. They complained that it kept them from being able to be social, or from being able to discuss and pray about issues they thought were important, both to them personally and to the church as a whole. Mark was at a loss as to how to respond to what he saw as a challenge to his authority. These groups were becoming like little churches, and he could sense an independent spirit that was pulling them away from his leadership.

As if that weren't enough, Mark also mentioned that Bob Newcomb, an elder on the church board who provided accounting advice to help Mark guide the church bookkeeper, had expressed concerns about the bookkeeper's ability to keep up with the volume and frequency of changes in tax and accounting rules. Bob was suggesting that the church may either need to hire a full-time business administrator, or contract with an accounting firm to provide a higher level of financial and administrative guidance. Mark was adamant that the church could not afford such a budget hit at this time, but he agreed with the basic issues Bob had raised. He just didn't have a good solution.

Next, George James, a long-time friend and financial supporter, asked Jerry to lunch. He was concerned about comments he was hearing from some of the newer members who also were significant supporters of the church's mission program, building fund, and other special projects. They were attracted to the dynamic atmosphere and preaching of the church and had committed resources and time to various ministries. But they went to George because they didn't feel they could get Jerry's ear. Every time one of them tried to approach the senior pastor, he seemed to be too busy or was interrupted by a higher priority problem. George understood their concerns and did his best to let them know how busy Jerry was, especially during the recently concluded building program. "But," he told Jerry, "I think these well-intentioned, loyal new members have a point. As I have prayed about it, I believe I have an idea that might help."

Jerry forced a smile and said, "Wow! That's a new one. Someone bringing a solution along with the problem. First time for everything!"

"Thanks for the sarcasm, Jerry," responded George with an even bigger smile. "But not only do I have a solution—I am willing to be a part of it."

Jerry resisted the temptation to continue kidding George, and instead got serious. "Tell me about it," he said.

George continued, "Well, what if I helped form a small group with some of these folks? We all have a common interest in seeing the church succeed and having a real impact on the community. I would make sure it doesn't turn into a gripe or gossip session disguised as prayer requests. We would use the curriculum pastor Mark is providing, but I would orient the application of biblical principles to current church issues as well as to the personal issues of the group."

"But wouldn't that seem like manipulation?" countered Jerry.

"Hmm. Good point. Then I should really be up front, I suppose, about the purpose of the group. Maybe we could look at it as a group of 'armor-bearers' and let that be our special interest. Mark has encouraged new groups to form around various common interests, so that could be ours. Wow. I just thought of that. What do you think, Pastor?"

Jerry looked thoughtful and said, "That's good. I could come to the group every couple of months and let them know what's on my heart as well as listen to them. That would also help hold them accountable to being loyal to the ministry. I could redirect any weird ideas they might have into areas that support our goals. We have to make sure that influential people like them don't go off on tangents that can confuse other church members."

"Well, I hope that's not their motive, but I see your point. When do you think we could start this group?"

Jerry replied, "Talk to Mark, but I don't see any reason to delay. Maybe I could meet with them before my sabbatical this summer. The elders on the church board and I have scheduled a couple of prayer times about this, but I think a group of newer members will provide a fresh intensity and perspective. Let's do it." Then he added, "I'm glad you are getting in front of potential problems like this. Thanks, my friend."

George was puzzled by Jerry's suspicious comments about the group, but he let it go and decided to focus on the positives. He extended both hands and took Jerry by the shoulders. He looked into his eyes and said, "Pastor, God is going to use the next few months, and particularly your sabbatical, to take this church to a new level. I know it in my spirit. I am committed to doing everything I can to help you realize the fullness of God's design for your life and ministry." Months of accumulated stress began to wash away as Jerry could feel the tears coming. "George, you have no idea how much I needed this. You are a true friend. God bless you and your family."

On his way home, Jerry thought about the trials of the past few weeks and the way George's encouragement helped him finally have some hope. The more he thought about it, though, he began to wonder about Mark's, and even George's, motives. "Sure, they seem to be trying to help. Mark wants to establish his authority, both with the small groups and with the church finances, but is he going about it the right way? What is he really saying? Maybe he is implying that I am not giving him the authority or resources he should have to get his job done. Maybe he thinks I should be doing more to back him up. Does he really trust me?

"And George. He's a great guy, but he is very influential in the church. Could this new small group be a way to extend his influence with these up and coming new members? Good thing I asked to drop in on them to keep an eye on what they are doing. Maybe one of the things I need to work on during the sabbatical is a thorough assessment of my staff and leaders, and their loyalty to this ministry and to me. Yes, I have to be careful not to get so caught up in personal relationships that I don't see the big picture. I have to make sure I've got the right people in the right slots."

# 3

## The Family Vacation

When he arrived home, Jerry determined to approach the issue of the family vacation energetically, in spite of the heaviness he felt from the problems at the church. Surely, if he could deal with complex church issues, a family vacation should not be too hard. With unaccustomed boldness, Jerry waded in to the vacation planning topic. He first briefed Donna on his thoughts, and then called a family meeting. "OK," he started, "we need to figure out how to make this the most fun and exciting family vacation EVER!" He was met with hopeful, but silent smiles.

Stephanie was the first to respond. "Dad, everyone wants to do something different. We all prayed separately over the past couple of weeks, but it doesn't seem that God is helping us come together on a location. Steve is still set on New Zealand, which we all know is impractical. Don has this thing for Spain. Who knows why, but he's being a teenage boy about it. I just want to have a fun and exciting trip to Florida. We always go to see family on vacations, so just this once, why can't we go to Disney World, EPCOT, and Universal Studios like everyone else in America has done? I've used a trip planning app to find the best deals on hotel and ticket packages. It's a no-brainer."

"Yeah," said Steve, "you always know best! Right. Everybody goes to Florida. The crowds and lines are legendary. That's exactly why we need to do something different. New Zealand is so cool! Did you know a lot of famous movies were shot there? How cool would it be to see the Shire from *Lord of the Rings*? I mean, I don't know anyone who has done that."

Don chimed in, "Are you kidding, Steve? Do you know how long it takes to get to New Zealand, and how much it would cost? It's an island in the middle of nowhere. What else is there to see but a bunch of scenery? Big deal. If we are going to fly, let's go somewhere exciting, like Spain. Didn't you like that YouTube special on the running of the bulls in Pompeii, or wherever? We never get to do anything fun. It's always what is practical and economical. I'm ready for something different!"

"Pamplona!" said Stephanie, wearily. "Is that all you care about, watching other people running for their lives? What fun," she said as she rolled her eyes.

Finally, Donna cleared the air with a solemn statement, "Ok! Your father has a plan for making this decision. Would you like to hear it?" One by one, Stephanie, Don, and Steve reluctantly agreed.

"OK, Dad," said Stephanie, "what's this great plan? Another trip to the cousins? A staycation?"

"Stephanie, I'm glad you asked that question." Challenged by another eye roll from his oldest, Jerry continued. "Well, it's very simple. Since we have not been able to come to agreement, the plan is for me, as the father and leader of this family, to make a wise decision that everyone will come to love. Seriously, I think I know what will make everybody happy. I heard about a family camping adventure. It has the natural beauty of New Zealand, the excitement of the bulls of Spain, and fun rides of Disney World. Plus, it will be a whole lot cheaper than any of those, and it will be closer to home in case any emergencies come up at the church."

The silence was deafening. Stephanie was the first to speak. "Uh, exactly what are we talking about?"

Jerry described to them a new water park that had opened the previous year. It was in their state, and near another big ride entertainment complex. He described the adjacent state park with cabins overlooking a lake well-known for fishing and watersports. "It'll be great! We'll have a full kitchen and cook all your favorite foods. There's even a fire pit for hot dogs, hamburgers, and toasted marshmallows."

Stephanie whined, "Do you know anyone who has been to this place? And who is the 'we' who are going to cook these fabulous meals?"

"Well, I don't know anyone personally, but the reviews I saw on the Internet looked good. And this will be a great opportunity for everyone to pitch in as a family, me included. I'll get a recipe for gourmet macaroni and cheese that everyone will love!"

"Wonderful. Are we going to spend the whole two weeks at this place?" said Don.

"You bet! There is so much to do and see. Besides, if you spend more than 7 days at the cabin, I think they throw in a 4-wheeler adventure for everyone. Four hours of exciting trails and an awesome fresh-caught trout lunch by the lake. Doesn't that sound great?"

Steve chimed in, "Well, if you say so. The macaroni and cheese sure sounds good, anyway. And I've always wanted to drive a 4-wheeler."

"That's the spirit. We'll have a blast, you'll see."

As they were leaving the family room, Stephanie pulled Don aside. "I don't get it. What's with Dad? I think work is getting to him. I thought this was supposed to be a family decision. Sounds to me like he just threw this together a few minutes before leaving for home. Really? A camping vacation where we all have to cook and do dishes? I haven't seen him this controlling since the building program. He just rolled over us. Here we go again. We preacher's kids have to grin and bear it, right?"

"You got it, Sis! But what did you expect? Our vacations are always about what he wants to do. That's why we go see Mom's relatives all the time. Then he gets to read and work on sermons while we have to entertain cousins and eat weird food.

"You saw how the church is still number one priority. We gotta be close enough if there is an emergency. Wow! There was never a chance for New Zealand, Spain, or even Orlando. Might as well stay home. At least we would have our friends around when things get boring."

As the family vacation and sabbatical approached, Jerry's weeks continued to be consumed with the normal cycle of preparing for Sunday's and Wednesday's messages, coordinating the next men's group meeting, staff issues, administrative approvals, and consultations with church members on a host of topics. In addition, he had to finalize arrangements for covering all of his responsibilities during the four weeks of time off. Finally, the vacation was about to become a reality. Stephanie and Donna had just returned from the Brazil missions trip, full of excitement about the unexpected encounters with members of the local church during the day and about the people who came to know Jesus in the evening outreach meetings.

Donna had prepared the menus and shopping list for the two-week camping trip, and Jerry and the boys had spent all of one morning at the grocery store stocking up on food, sunscreen, insect repellent, new swimsuits, and water toys. She quickly realized that a lot was left to be done at the last minute, and was beginning to realize that this wasn't going to be much of a "vacation" for her. She kept her thoughts to herself, determined to make this a memorable time for the kids. The contrast with her excitement and fulfillment during the missions trip, though, was telling. She decided, one more time, to suck it up and be the obedient pastor's wife. But deep in her heart she cried out, "Lord, are things ever going to change? Is this all I have to look forward to the rest of my life? Being a dutiful pastor's wife? You know I'm willing to sacrifice everything for You. But somehow I believe there is more. Much more. Help me believe, and show me how to pray for our family and for this man You have called me to love."

The vacation was a whirlwind of activities and home-cooked meals with the whole family dutifully at the table for breakfast and dinner. Donna was grateful for the time Jerry was able to spend with the kids. She bent over backwards to fix healthy meals, and always had a favorite dish of at least one child. Without intending to, she and Jerry fell into the pattern of him taking the kids to theme park rides and camp activities, while she stayed back to clean up from one meal and prepare the next. She told herself that she was happy to do this, but as the days passed, she realized that she was resentful that she was missing out on these family experiences. The kids eventually seemed to be having a good time, so she continued to hold back her feelings and put on a happy face when they would return to tell about the 4-wheeler ride, the river float trip, and more.

What Donna didn't see was the interaction between her husband and the kids during these outings. She didn't see that he continued to make all the decisions and diplomatically work around their suggestions. For example, he reluctantly splurged on the horseback ride, but when Stephanie began to really enjoy it and asked to guide if she could gallop for a bit, Jerry interrupted and said that it wouldn't be safe since this was her first time on a horse. Don especially grew more and more sullen. While he enjoyed most of the rides and activities, he inwardly resented not having a say in what they did. He once more felt that he was expected to just sit back and enjoy this pre-programmed "adventure."

As the vacation came to a close, Donna determined to seek the Lord in prayer while Jerry was on his sabbatical. She knew that in spite of the additional load she was taking on over the next two weeks, with paying bills, house and lawn maintenance, and summer sports, that she could trust God to see her heart and answer her prayer. "God, change me! Give me grace and patience to acknowledge Your hand in all of this busyness. I choose to rest in Your goodness and mercy. Heal my offended heart and my wounded family. I release Jerry to You. I release my expectations to You. I release my rights to You. I am Yours."

# 4

# The Sabbatical Begins

As Jerry began the second part of his sabbatical, he realized the vacation had been fun, but also physically and emotionally exhausting. He had felt compelled to plan every moment with activities for the kids and to participate to the max. It had been a real stretch to find things they could all do, and to put up with the complaints when not everyone wanted to do everything. But he was determined to fill the time and make lasting memories. So he was grateful that George James had arranged for him to spend most of the next two weeks at an isolated lake cabin. While he had no idea that Donna was even more exhausted from the "vacation," Jerry was also grateful that George thoughtfully arranged for Donna to have a housekeeper twice a week during the sabbatical.

Donna originally was supposed to join Jerry on one of the Saturdays, but she felt that being with Jerry was the last place she needed to be, and insisted on him spending the entire time away from them. Maybe she would have enough time by herself to recover from the resentment she had about having full responsibility for the cooking and housekeeping during the camping trip. Once again, she decided to be silent. She told him that he should devote himself to pray, read, write in a journal, take long walks, and try to catch fish for as many of his dinners as possible. Jerry agreed, having no idea about Donna's feelings.

On the Sundays during his sabbatical, Jerry found some churches near the lake with different types of services that he could slip into without anyone knowing who he was. He wanted to get fresh ideas about how

God was meeting other congregations that were very different from his own. During the week, his focus was on examining the various aspects of his church's ministries and on researching past moves of God. Overall, his goal was, in spite of his personal misgivings, to "prepare for revival," as the Holy Spirit had directed him several months earlier.

"God," prayed Jerry earnestly the morning after his arrival, "what do You want to show me during these two weeks? I want to make the best use of the time, so I need to hear Your priorities, Your heart." He had a dream that night about an incident from his childhood. He was walking to school with a friend, and a much older student came alongside them. The bully made fun of them both, laughing at their clothes and threatening to take their coats and throw them in a dumpster, "where they belonged." Jerry looked at his friend and yelled, "Run!" They ran all the way to school, with the bully shouting "Scaredy cats! Mommy's boys!" They stayed far away from the bully the rest of the day. The dream ended with Jerry telling his mom about it that night, but she just laughed and said, "Boys will be boys. It was just words. You didn't get hurt. Forget about it." Jerry woke up feeling the same shame and embarrassment he had felt from that incident and others like it. He could not go back to sleep and sat outside on the porch, looking at the stars. He had worked hard all his life to overcome feelings of inadequacy, and now, just when he was asking God to show him how to go to the next level, these childhood fears came flooding back. "God, what does this mean? I've put this behind me years ago. Why is this coming back now? I was just a kid then. I'm a man. I'm not afraid of anyone. It doesn't seem fair."

Then Jerry heard a quiet voice inside him whisper, "No, Jerry, it isn't fair. Hurts from the past are not fair. You didn't do anything to deserve that. But the devil has allowed you to relive that shame over and over. Even when you haven't thought about it for a long time, the hurt still causes you to get angry or try to control people. It's time to put it behind you. Would you like to do that?"

"Yes, of course, Lord," thought Jerry, almost out loud. "What do I need to do?"

"I want you to talk to Mark about it."
"Mark, my associate pastor? Why?"
Silence.
"I said, why Mark? What would I say? Men don't talk about stuff like that. Why should I?"
Long silence.
"OK, I get it. I'm just supposed to be obedient, right? OK, I'll do it, but I'm not going to like it. And Mark is going to think I'm weird for telling about these embarrassing incidents from the ancient past."

Mark was scheduled to come to the cabin in a couple of days to fish, to pray, and to discuss his ministry areas with Jerry. It promised to be a very fruitful time. Jerry always admired Mark's talents and energy. He would tackle any problem and stick with it until it was resolved. Jerry was looking forward to challenging Mark to seek the Holy Spirit for direction and see him grow in spiritual awareness. He saw Mark's potential to be not just a good pastor and administrator, but to be a mighty man of God. But now, why throw in this personal baggage from the past? "Oh well," sighed Jerry. "Like David dancing before the ark, I guess I can make myself a fool for the Lord if I have to."

For the next two days, Jerry got down to business with his research into past revivals, or "moves of God" as he preferred to say it, unconsciously avoiding the "R" word. He had brought several books that dealt with the subject, and his cellular internet connection in the cabin was surprisingly strong, so he was able to find good online resources as well. One of the first things he noticed was that each move was led by a man of God with a supernatural anointing who practiced persistent prayer and a holy lifestyle. This confirmed his decision to go deeper into spiritual intimacy, for his own sake, but also to set an example for his associates and lay leaders. It was obvious from history that God could use anyone who was fully yielded to Him, and that unusual oratorical skills, planning and organization, or showmanship were not always critical – just extreme devotion to the things of God.

He learned a number of other lessons from the history of revivals beginning with the Great Awakenings of the 18th and 19th centuries in

America, Britain, and elsewhere, through the Welsh Revival, Azusa Street outpouring, and Pentecostal/charismatic waves of the 20th century, ending with the Argentina, Toronto and Pensacola, revivals. Jerry noted that some of the lessons were as follows:

- The primary result was to save souls and make zealous disciples in large numbers.
- Those who humbly seek God with deep and persistent prayer are honored by Him with gifts and power, even when the person has serious weaknesses that eventually hurt the ministry.
- Many persevered in spite of persecution, sickness, poverty, and shame. They often overcame severe family dysfunction and hard circumstances in early life. We should not pass over weaknesses lightly, but learn from them. We want to be similarly motivated, but also have a healthy foundation from which to approach God so that the results of His favor can be sustained.
- Many focused on personal conviction and confession of sin, sincere repentance, the fear of God's judgment, and developing a heart completely sold out to seeing the Kingdom of God revealed on earth.
- In some cases, a revival was activated through a period of dedicated private and congregational prayer and fasting.
- Revival was often spread as the news of a revival reached other parts of the world, causing increased faith, anticipation, and prayer for the same anointing to fall. Many pastors and missionaries would also come from around the world to revival centers to receive an impartation from the Holy Spirit and carry it back to their home churches.
- While revivalists exhibited a variety of styles, from minimalist (Jonathan Edwards) to flamboyant (Billy Sunday, Aimee Semple McPherson, and Katherine Kuhlman), most demonstrated a clear and thoughtful exposition of the Word, whether carefully prepared or extemporaneous. One of the most effective, Charles Haddon

Spurgeon, wrote his sermons out, but then spoke from an outline on note cards. He finally edited for publication the transcriptions of his messages as delivered. His writings are among the all-time best-selling sermon series.
- Some focused on personal holiness and evangelism, whereas others focused on supernatural manifestations of healing and prophetic words, resulting in conviction in the hearts of their listeners. Many skeptics, religious and secular, when confronted with God's power, humbled themselves and were converted and filled with the Holy Spirit.
- The most effective characteristic of revivalists is for others to see God in them, so that it is not so much the words they say, but the spirit they convey that attracts and impacts the hearts of their hearers. (John G. Lake said this of William Seymour of the Azusa Street revival.)
- Some, but by no means all, stressed being accountable within small groups of interconnected, praying believers. This was probably one of the most important factors in seeing long term fruits from a period of revival. The consistent prayer by organized small groups of the Moravians starting in 1727 lasted over a hundred years.
- A few revivalists, especially those who spent a lot of time in prayer, would wait on the Holy Spirit to move in His way and timing, with little concern for a programmed agenda or length of service.
- Most effective revivals were accompanied by worship with anointed singing and instruments.
- Some revivals, as in Argentina during the 1990s, were birthed out of dire circumstances such as natural disasters, military defeat, or financial upheaval, causing the people to cry out for relief from God.

Jerry also kept a list of the factors that seemed to cause revivals to wane, or even to fall apart, such as:

- In some cases divisions and jealousies arose among leaders, especially where there was not a single dominant leader. Often, divisions were caused by differences in theology. This almost aborted the Moravian movement, but Count Zinzendorf learned to come together on areas of agreement rather than trying to resolve differences.
- The strong, dominant leader brought cohesiveness and excitement to many revival movements. However, personal notoriety and focus on large numbers of salvations resulted in the leader moving from place to place. Few emphasized small groups and local churches to continue the work of discipling new believers.
- Other, more insidious, problems with the strong leader model were:
  o the temptation to see one's anointing as an excuse to treat staff as mere tools to obtain the ministry's ever more demanding goals, and even to take advantage of the financial rewards
  o pride and an unteachable spirit, forgetting the humility that allowed God's grace to bring revival in the first place
  o holiness and sanctification taken to extremes, leading to legalism instead of freedom. For example, Evan Roberts, and to some degree William Seymour, were obsessed with examining themselves and others for unconfessed sin, which eventually created a religious spirit of legalism and shame rather than hope in a loving God of grace and mercy
- From Lee Grady, Charisma, 2006, on the Brownsville revival in Pensacola
  o History shows us that revival is always risky. The devil opposes it, and carnal flesh gets in the way of it. The Holy Spirit is easily quenched by pride, greed, selfish religious agendas, and broken relationships (among leaders).
  o For those in Pensacola who were swept up in the ecstasy of those early years, and then endured splits, resignations, debts, and disappointments, the word "revival" now has a hollow

ring to it. Still, my heart cries: "Lord, do it again." Next time He does, I pray we will carry the ark the way God intended—and keep our hands off of it.

Jerry got excited as he developed a deeper appreciation for how God moves during periods of revival. He realized that it requires sacrificial commitment, discipline, and absolute hunger for God, not just for himself, but for those around him who are going to help steward whatever God wants to do. This last bullet, however, was sobering. Even in modern times, he thought, with all of our knowledge and study of history, we still are able to get swept up into circumstances and behaviors that can quench God's moving.

He decided that he would put the research notes aside and review them occasionally, but that he was not about to try to plan for a move of God until he knew he had his own spiritual house in order. That meant seeking God with every fiber of his being and having healthy, loving relationships with everyone around him. With that, he began to pray about his time tomorrow with his associate pastor, Mark Henson. This was a great opportunity to go deeper with an important relationship, not just for the ministry, but for him personally.

"Lord, I see Your heart for revival. It's not about the ministry at all. It's about our relationships to You and to one another. Touch me now through Your Holy Spirit. Go deep inside and heal my heart so I can give it wholly to You, to my wife and family, and to my friends. I don't know what this looks like, but I humble myself before You and these precious saints. Fill me with Your sacrificial love, the love You have within the Godhead – between the Father, the Son, and the Holy Spirit. You loved me so much that You gave Your Son's very life. Now You have given me Your Holy Spirit to show me the way to give my heart, my life, for You and others."

As Jerry continued to pour out his heart before the Father, he was overcome with emotion. Tears began to flow, and he dropped to the ground in humility and worship. The Holy Spirit brought to his mind the bullying incidents and showed him how to bring this up with Mark. Where there was confusion and doubt about this two days ago, he was now confident that he could step out in faith and God would somehow use this to answer his prayers for deeper intimacy. He just needed to be obedient.

# 5

## Mark and Breakthrough

When Mark arrived the next morning, Jerry was preparing a heavy breakfast.

"Mark, glad you are here. We have a lot to do and pray about today, so I wanted to get off to a good start. How do you like your eggs?"

As the bacon was frying, Jerry asked Mark about his family, and the two men compared light-hearted stories of the stresses they were feeling in balancing the demands of their wives, children, and the ministry.

"Pastor, I envy you in being able to get away from everything, even if just for a few weeks. Does it get any easier, you know, keeping everyone happy at home and at the church? My wife just doesn't seem to understand the pressures and time I have to spend at the church. I'm not complaining about that. I love the challenges and sense of helping so many people. I wish she were a little more understanding and supportive, though."

"I know what you mean. I thought it would get easier with time, but it really doesn't. I think that's why this sabbatical is so important to me. We all need time to stop and reflect, and to figure out our priorities. I'm hoping Donna will take this time to think about what all I have to deal with as well. Perhaps being apart for a couple of weeks will help us both appreciate one another more. But tell me how your little girl is doing? How old is she now?"

The two men continued talking about family, the latest softball game, and funny stories about church members. As they finished sopping up the last of the biscuits and gravy, Jerry turned the casual conversation to a serious note. "Mark, what really motivates you to do your best for God?"

"Pastor, I know it's early in the morning, but I really have been praying about this time with you. I feel that I can do my best for God by praying and listening to what He is saying each day. I have to confess that I am a morning person, so I'm pretty pumped after driving here early and having a big breakfast. I heard in the car on the way that I am to listen carefully and be honest in stating my thoughts. So there you are! What's next?"

"You make me laugh, Mark. I don't have a specific agenda. I just want to hear from you about yourself, your family, and your areas of ministry, how things are going, and what you would like to see happen in the next few months and even years, if you can look that far out."

With that open door, Mark pulled out a notebook and opened to a list of bullet points. "Well, we've talked about me and my family, but I do have a few thoughts about the ministry," he grinned. Jerry and he discussed some of the current issues and upcoming events, particularly the problem with the small groups who were wanting to do their own thing. Jerry listened to some of the details, and then asked Mark a question. "What do you think is behind the need for some of the groups to be more independent?"

"Well, I really hadn't thought about that," said Mark hesitantly. "I guess I assumed they just wanted to do things their own way. Maybe they think my curriculum is boring. I don't know."

"Mark, why don't we pray about this right now? There may be more to it than either of us realize."

The two men finished praying, and then waited for a couple of minutes in silence to hear what the Holy Spirit might be saying. Finally, Mark opened his eyes and almost shouted, "I know what it is! At least with two of the groups, they have members who are going through some tough trials, some with sickness and others with dysfunctional family situations. I think they want to focus on these issues and spend quality time in prayer and encouragement. It's not about the material at all. They just have other needs at this time."

Jerry joined in, "Well, then, here's a solution that might work. Why don't you attend each of those groups once over the next few months to show your support and to pray for their needs? As they see you moving towards them, let's trust the Holy Spirit to work in their lives, bring healing, and then gently guide them back to your vision for the small groups. As you serve them, they will want to return your investment of love."

"And even if they don't," chuckled Mark, "maybe by then I will have some more interesting and interactive topics in the material. You know, I've been thinking about allowing more flexibility in the meeting agendas. Perhaps they should be able to use the study guides as just that, guides, and not feel that they have to work through one every meeting. Especially if there are pressing prayer needs, as I know these two groups have."

"Mark, that's great thinking. It's amazing how the Holy Spirit works on all sides of an issue, isn't it?"

After discussing a few more of Mark's points, including some long range goals, Jerry poured another cup of coffee for each of them. He sat down, looked Mark straight in the eyes, and said, "This is a bit awkward, Mark, but I feel I'm supposed to confide something in you. I don't know why, but I can't ignore it."

"Sure, Pastor. Go ahead. I'm all ears. Seriously, what is it?"

"Well, Mark, at the beginning of my time here, I asked the Lord to show me His heart. I wanted to make sure there wasn't anything in me that was hindering my intimacy with Him. I really want to grow closer to Him during this time away and hear His heart for me, my family, and the church.

"Totally unexpected, I had a dream that night about a bullying incident when I was in middle school. A number of things like that happened during those years that caused me a lot of embarrassment and shame. I hadn't thought about it in a long time, but apparently it is still causing me issues that need to be resolved. Even more embarrassing, I clearly heard the Holy Spirit say that I was to talk to you about it. Believe me, I have no idea what's going on with this. But I've put too much prayer time into this sabbatical to not do what I believe I am supposed to do."

Jerry recounted the incidents, how they made him feel, and the interactions he had with his parents about it. Then he paused for a few seconds, unable to find any clues from Mark's face about what he was thinking. "So that's it," he finally continued. "Am I crazy, or what?"

Mark's expression and body language were impenetrable. After almost a minute of focusing on the wall, he pushed back his chair, stood up, and walked to the window overlooking the nearby lake where they were going fishing later in the day. As he gazed at the beautiful scene, he said very deliberately, not turning around to look at Jerry, "Pastor, you have no idea what this means to me."

After another uncomfortable period of silence, Mark moved to an easy chair in the living area, where Jerry joined him with two cups of coffee. As Mark accepted the fresh cup, and Jerry sat down on the facing sofa, Mark continued, "I don't know where to begin. I completely understand what you mean about embarrassment and shame following you from something that happened in childhood. I have to confess a very dark secret myself. I have never told anyone besides my wife. It happened the first time when I was six. An older cousin molested me in the woods behind our house while his family was staying with us for a few days. I was very confused and didn't know what to do. He threatened me, of course, and said that he would beat me up if I told anyone. I didn't, but the next time the family visited us, a year later, he did the same thing and threatened me even more severely. I was terrified and ashamed. I had nightmares off and on over the next few years.

"Finally, when I was around 11 and the cousins were planning another visit, I told my mom that I really didn't want them to come. When she pressed me for a reason, I hesitated, and then decided to tell her a half-truth. I said that he had touched me where he shouldn't have the last several times they were here, and that I was afraid of him. My mom made light of it, I suppose since she and her sister were very close. She said she would find somewhere else I could go that weekend if that would make me feel better. I agreed, but we never talked about it again. She never asked me any more questions, and never told my Dad, as far as I know.

"I was able to avoid my cousin while I was still at home, but since then, family reunions have been very uncomfortable for me. My cousin acts as though I don't exist. I have never brought up the past except to tell Sarah before we were married so she could understand and help me avoid being around him if at all possible. She was very sympathetic, of course. But I can tell that it is a source of disappointment and shame for her as well. She does not like to acknowledge it much less talk about it anymore."

Jerry got up slowly and went to the same window. He said very quietly, "Mark, I am so sorry. I had no idea." He was beginning to see that his frank confession was part of God's plan to bring Mark and him closer together, as well as to help Mark get free from this weight; however, he was surprised that it would be over such personal things. His pastor's instinct took over, and he knew he had to move towards the situation, and towards Mark, in this sensitive moment.

He decided to take the spotlight off of Mark and put it back on himself. "I can't imagine how that must have made you feel all these years. I know it has been a struggle for me to overcome the insecurities and shame from being bullied. I thought I had left it behind, but I still get angry when I think about it."

Mark did not respond, other than to look straight at him, so Jerry continued. "Just the other day I said something to Donna that I regretted. She asked me to do something that I thought she had already taken care of. I got upset and told her that if she had done what she promised, it wouldn't have got to the point that I needed to step in. Well, that didn't sit well with her, and before I knew it we were raising our voices and both saying things we shouldn't have."

"You think that has something to do with your being bullied in school? I don't get it."

"I don't know. It's more than a coincidence that I am asking to go deeper with God, and then this sets off some hidden source of anger. I think there could be a connection. I haven't let anything get to me like that since the tree-trimming incident."

With that, Mark chuckled out loud, and both men began to relax as they recounted the unfortunate run-in with the utility company. Mark seemed to have forgotten about his confession, but then he was quiet for a while, and finally said suddenly, "Pastor, I think I get it. And I think it explains some things that have been going on in my life."

"OK, Mark," said Jerry hesitantly. "Let's hear it."

"Well," Mark continued almost enthusiastically, "at first I was thinking your anger is just from having to stuff your resentment towards the bully all those years ago. But then I realized that probably wasn't as big a deal as what happened with your parents."

"My parents? What do they have to do with it?"

"Maybe it's a stretch, but didn't you mention that they downplayed the incident and didn't really come to your defense? Like my mom not taking my situation seriously, or even telling my dad."

"Yes, that's right," admitted Jerry. "I just figured it was something I had to deal with."

"That's exactly what I went through. I never really trusted my mom afterwards. Did their not taking your situation seriously change how you related to your parents afterwards?"

"I suppose so. Yes, I guess I decided that I would have to take care of business myself and not rely on them or others to protect me. I hadn't thought about that, but I did become pretty independent, even at that young age. I learned to dish it out when people even hinted at trying to take advantage of me. I rarely told my parents about such things. I just took care of it myself. But what does that have to do with my anger towards my wife, the tree-trimmers, or even towards the bullies when I think about it?"

"Maybe," suggested Mark, "just maybe the anger is not towards those people, but it is in response to the fear that has gone deep in your own soul."

"Fear? What fear? If anything I've learned not to be afraid of anyone."

"Not fear of them," said Mark calmly, sensing that he was being led by the Holy Spirit to step out boldly. "Fear of not being in control. Fear that people are not looking out for your safety, like your parents. Fear that they have power over your property, like the tree-trimmers. And fear that they can't be trusted to keep their promises, like your wife."

Jerry stopped cold, like he had been hit with a two-by-four. "I don't know. Maybe. I have to think about it," he said. Then he corrected himself, "No, I don't have to think about it. I have to pray about it. Let's do that right now."

Jerry paused and prayed a simple request for wisdom, for the Holy Spirit to reveal the deep fears and anxieties of his heart. Mark joined in and prayed for Jerry, but also for himself, that he would have the same wisdom and that God would likewise search his heart.

After both men were lost in contemplation for a few minutes, Jerry finally opened his eyes. "Mark, you are absolutely right. This is an amazing insight. It all started with my reaction to my parents. I no longer trusted them to take care of me, so I began to learn to take care of myself. And I truly don't trust others in my life to this very day, even my wife, who is just trying to help me in every way she can. And the issue with your small groups. I have to admit that I was having to suppress the feeling that these folks are just resisting your authority, and that reflects on me. Our solution a few minutes ago was inspired, but it was not my first thought. I can't believe I have been so blind to what has been causing these inner thoughts and outward reactions. What do I do now?"

"You got me, Pastor. I'm in overload unpacking what the trauma I experienced as a child has done to me, my friends, my wife, and my ministry. I thought I had suppressed it pretty well, but I see now that it controls so much of my reactions and emotions, or lack thereof. No wonder Sarah says to me all the time that I need to be more open with my emotions. I have been stuffing them for so long that I don't know how I really feel anymore."

"Boy, Mark, we are a mess!" said Jerry with a smile. "It's going to take a big God to clean us up. Good thing we have a big God, huh?"

"You are so right about that, Pastor. What's our next step?"

"I think we should 'go a-fishing', as a great apostle once said."

"Yep, just before Jesus showed up and healed Peter's heart. Let's go!"

The two men spent several hours in a canoe with light tackle, catching an occasional sand bass. They talked about sports, upcoming ministry events, and Jerry's experiences at the family camping vacation. As they were paddling back to the dock to clean their fish for lunch, Jerry picked back up on the morning's conversation. "Mark, what do you think about staying a little longer this afternoon to write down what we discussed this morning and see where that takes us? I know many other men must have similar things in their past but never talk about it. Maybe we should figure out a way to work through these issues and set an example for the men in our church."

"OK, I'm willing to give it a shot. It can't be an accident that we are spending time on this during your sabbatical. God has set us up for a blessing, I'm sure. It just feels a little strange, though. I certainly wasn't planning to get into this touch-feely stuff. I'm much more comfortable cleaning fish, planning events, and solving problems."

"Yeah, me too. I guess this is kind of like solving problems. Only it's our personal problems. Maybe it's like the flight attendant says – put your oxygen mask on yourself first before you put it on your child. Maybe we need to go through this before we try it on others."

"Well, I have an idea," replied Mark. "After lunch, let's put down our thoughts in the form of a letter to the person who hurt us. I think I remember someone talking about doing that at an inner healing conference. We wouldn't give it to them, of course. It would just be to get our feelings out there so God can deal with them. Like Job did. Like David. God wanted them to say what was hurting them. I could write a letter to my cousin, for example, and you could write one to the worst of the bullies who shamed you."

Jerry struck a thoughtful pose for a minute or so. Mark resisted the urge to ask him what he was thinking. Finally, Jerry said, "You know, Mark, I don't think I should write it to the bully. I think I want to write it to my father."

"Why? Aren't we supposed to forgive the ones who hurt us? Your father didn't do anything."

"Yes, but he didn't stand up for me. He told me to be tough and not let them get away with it. But he didn't do anything about it. I didn't want to disappoint him, so from then on I didn't tell anyone when I was bullied. I just did the best I could to avoid them. But that was the beginning of not trusting my dad to help me. I may have gotten over the fear of being intimidated by others, but I withdrew from my dad, not letting him know about other problems I had. We really grew apart over the years, and even today we have a very superficial relationship. No, he's the one who really hurt me. I don't even remember the names of most of the bullies. They are just ugly faces who didn't mean anything to me besides the shame and fear that I felt."

Mark's face and posture grew more tense as Jerry spoke. He quickly said, "Well, it's my cousin who violated me. I may have said a prayer of forgiveness for him a while back, but I still have trouble letting it go, and the feelings of bitterness and hatred for him are as strong as ever. In fact, the more I think about it, I believe I would do him bodily harm if I had the chance and thought I could get away with it. I'm sorry to say that, but it's how I feel. I'm definitely feeling the need to have it out with him, even if it's just in a letter. Then maybe I can really forgive him and put it behind me. I have to do something. It is beginning to have a major impact on my relationship with my wife."

After a man-sized late lunch of fried fish, hushpuppies, and coleslaw, Mark and Jerry each took a spiral notebook and began to write their letters. Jerry sat on the porch while the sun was dropping towards the western tree line around the lake. Mark walked down the path to a picnic table. They each asked God to help them, as David asked in Psalm 139 to "search me and know my heart and anxieties." When they came back together, they read their letters to each other. Jerry found that he thought of several other areas where his father had not supported and protected him. His letter didn't blame his father as much as it showed Jerry's heart of wanting that support, or as he began to realize, that love from his father. He realized that he never remembered hearing his father say that he loved him. The more he wrote, the more angry and hurt he felt. He finally realized that he could not actually write the words of forgiveness to his father.

When Jerry admitted this, Mark said, "Wait until you hear my letter. When I prayed, I imagined my cousin's face, leering at me once again, and threatening me if I told anyone. If he had walked out from behind a tree right then, I think I would have strangled him. I was shocked at the rage in my gut. Then a strange thing happened. I was so unnerved by the murder within me, that I remembered Christ's words during the Sermon on the Mount. It was probably on a hillside much like I was seeing, leading down to the lake. He said that if we have hatred towards someone it was the same as murdering them. I felt that hatred, and I felt that desire to murder. I mean, it was so real. But when those words came back to me, I fell on the ground and asked God to forgive me for the sin of hatred and bitterness I had bottled up all these years. I felt His loving touch, forgiving me and washing my sin away, just like when I was saved. The next words out of my mouth were, 'I forgive my cousin.' As bad as his sin was, mine was worse."

Jerry's mouth had dropped open as Mark spoke. When he slowly closed it and swallowed hard, he said, "Oh my God! I mean oh God, forgive me for my sin towards my father! Here I am a pastor and have not made any attempt to reconcile with him. We may be civil to one another, but I've held anger in my heart towards him. I don't think I really understood why I felt so detached from him, but now I know it was my unforgiveness. I may have said general words of forgiveness, but I didn't really understand the depth of feeling that I had. I really need to ask forgiveness from him and from God. I can finally say that I forgive him sincerely from my heart."

For the next hour, the two men discussed what had just happened. They recognized the importance of what they had experienced, and they also saw that it was purely Holy Spirit led. From the first step of obedience Jerry took to reveal to Mark what he thought was an insignificant incident in the distant past, to the series of mutual disclosures, and finally to the incredibly deep and unexpectedly intimate experiences that touched their souls, both men knew that an eternal transaction had taken place. However, they also knew that they had just begun the first step of a supernatural journey, first of healing within their own souls, and then restoration of relationships with others. They decided that they needed to pray to understand what this meant for their families and the church.

With that, Jerry went on to discuss the goals of Mark's ministry areas and how he might support Mark in fulfilling them. As they got into details, Jerry was surprised at how easily he was able to appreciate and encourage Mark, and even agree enthusiastically with his ideas.

# 6

## Going Deeper

After Mark left, Jerry realized that he was operating out of a much different place than normal. He no longer felt the need to analyze and critique Mark's ideas, even those that were a bit uncomfortable, such as loosening up the curriculum for adult education classes, and allowing teachers to submit ideas for what they would like to teach. He realized that something had happened in his heart. Was it related somehow to the revelation he had about his relationship to his father? Had he actually been healed of the need to be in control because he no longer had to worry about the bullies? Was he able finally to trust in a heavenly father to protect him and those he loved from the bullies? Were those bullies just the fears and anxieties of everyday life?

Jerry began to realize the magnitude of what had begun to happen to him. Healing the relationship with his earthly father had opened up a whole new relationship with his heavenly Father. He could really trust Him to take care of both the big problems and the little ones. Jerry felt a huge weight lift from his chest as these thoughts crystallized in his mind and then settled in his heart. He had known these things almost since he had become a Christian as a teenager. But he realized now that it was mainly head knowledge, and that his heart and his emotions were still in bondage to the fears that had planted themselves in those early years. They had never been recognized, much less dealt with. Now he knew that he knew that Daddy God was taking care of him. Now and forever.

The rest of the night, Jerry contemplated the wonders of God's goodness—that He would make Himself so real. He even went to the trouble to include another person so that they both would receive the same kind of experience and then have a special bond. What a marvelous God to orchestrate such details! It was one thing to know that God is capable of miracles. It was just overwhelming to see and feel how He could have an impact on a professional pastor with such a fresh measure of love and compassion.

It dawned on Jerry that this was exactly what he had prayed for prior to the sabbatical. He had wanted a deeper, more intimate walk with God. He had imagined that it would come through study, prayer, worship music, and crying out in desperation. He was surprised by the joy that had blindsided him through a simple act of realizing his sin of bitterness arising from a long-forgotten wound, and asking forgiveness.

But wait. Isn't that just what salvation is all about? Realizing sin, repenting, and accepting Christ's sacrifice that purchased our forgiveness? Sure, we do that every day, just as the Lord's Prayer commands. Yes, it was that same cycle that he had just repeated, but how was this different? Maybe it was that the sin had been hidden for so long and had become so toxic that it had infected areas of his life and emotions in ways and to a depth that even he didn't realize. Wow. That devil is subtle. Well, it's out in the open now. The light has shined in the darkness. Hallelujah!

Later that night, after falling asleep in exhaustion, Jerry awoke and felt that he was to get up and write down his thoughts. He got a new notebook that he had bought hoping to start a habit of journaling deeper spiritual insights. He thought, "This is as good a time as any to start." After praying to simply be led by the Holy Spirit, he began to write a prayer from his heart:

"Dear God, You are Mighty, Counselor, Prince of Peace, Everlasting Father, but You are also my Daddy. I love You so much. I fall at Your feet, but then You pick me up and set me in Your lap and let me dance on Your knees. I am just a child, trusting in Your strength and character. I know You will never leave me or forsake me. You work all things for my good, because I am called according to Your purpose. I can do all things through Christ because You strengthen me.

"Father, I have asked You for a more intimate relationship, and You have done more than I could ever ask or think. You have made me a son. You have called me by name and designed me from my mother's womb. Blessed be Your Name. Most High. Mighty God. Precious Lamb, sacrificed for my sins and my redemption to eternal life with You and Your family. I am so proud to be called by Your Name. I will never turn from following You. I will be faithful to call to You and then obey what You tell me to do. Here I am, Father. Your son, Jerry."

With that, Jerry sighed, partly in peace, partly instead of yawning, and began to put away his pen and journal. But then he felt a strong urge to listen to what the Holy Spirit might be speaking to his spirit. With boldness, he took his pen back up and wrote as he felt prompted by the Holy Spirit gently and lovingly.

"Jerry, you are indeed My son. I sacrificed My only begotten Son so that I could have many sons and daughters. I did this to have a family based on sacrificial love, agape. I wanted My sons and daughters to realize that I would do anything for them to protect them and see them reach the potential that I placed in them as I formed them in the womb. But even more, I wanted them to trust Me."

Jerry felt that he had to say out loud, "I would do anything for You, Lord." But then he realized that in this moment he would do so. But what about later, when he wasn't in the midst of a major spiritual high? Or if things weren't going his way. He wasn't so sure, so he whispered softly, "I'm sure I don't fully understand or appreciate what You mean by trusting You, Lord."

He once more began to write as he felt led by the still small voice of the Holy Spirit. "Will you trust Me to orchestrate the circumstances in your life for your good, even if it doesn't seem that way to you? Will you unconditionally love those who persecute you or tell lies about you behind your back? Will you trust Me to deal with your wife if you think she is not doing the right thing? These are the ways you would trust Me. Will you do that, Jerry?"

Jerry realized he was going to have to be totally honest. He continued to verbalize, "Wow. That's tough when You put it that way. I can say, sure, in my mind. But I have to be honest, in my heart I would probably have a hard time, at least initially. I would have to ask You in each of those situations to help me. I wouldn't want to say I was trusting You and not really feel it deep down inside. That would be hypocritical. But then, I know I can't always seem to control my emotions with my mind. I want to trust You with both. I want to love You with my whole heart, and mind, and strength. Help me be that whole person, Lord!"

Jerry deliberately stretched out full length on a rug in the middle of the room and continued to pour out his heart. He felt even more of the Father's love pouring into him as a silent, but real answer. Finally, he sat back up and began to write again.

"Father, I have learned a valuable lesson the past few hours. I know I can't depend on myself, but I can depend on You in every situation. I know that if I ask, You will be there to comfort and guide me. You will give me peace that passes all understanding. You will give me direction, sometimes through the small, still voice of the Holy Spirit. Other times it may be loud like a drill sergeant when it is critical to obey immediately. But even if I don't hear You in the moment, I know that You are still with me and guiding me through circumstances and through wise counsel from others.

"And sometimes You will allow me to follow my own heart. You trust me more than I trust myself! While my heart starts out evil, You are transforming my mind and heart every day as I meditate on Your Word, as I seek You for comfort and guidance, and as I try to trust and obey You. Even if I make mistakes or allow old habits to interfere, I know You will quickly forgive as I recognize and confess my sin and repent. By repent, I mean not just be sorry for what I've done or allowed in my soul, but that I truly desire not to let it happen again. I will resist the devil and he will flee from me. Greater are You in me than the devil who tries to influence me from the outside. I will call upon You in the instant I am tempted to sin, and You will give me strength to resist. I resolve to obey, even in the small things. I will not give the devil even the slightest space to work in my mind or heart."

Jerry slept very well that night. The next morning he wrote extensively in his journal, recalling the powerful lessons of the encounter with Mark, with his own past, and with God. He began to get ideas for a major sermon series on confronting forgiveness, and then another one on the importance of intimate relationships. He could feel the Holy Spirit directing his thoughts as he wrote out the words that were flowing from his spirit.

As he finished his writing, and his second cup of coffee, he started praying about his afternoon visit with Gabe Miller. He had been listening to one of Gabe's demo recordings of original songs. While they might not have been written for congregational choruses to be sung on Sunday morning, they ministered to his heart in a way he had not been expecting. The words were very personal and revealed a surprising level of intimacy with the Father. Or perhaps he was just now able to understand the emotional intensity of the lyrics and the music. He certainly had a new appreciation for Gabe's relationship with the Father and his spiritual maturity.

> 10/4/19 —
> Start with prayer on page 36. Reread often — daily if necessary. Maybe even hour by hour.

# 7

## Gabe and the Oberlins

As Gabe drove up after lunch, Jerry said a quick prayer for guidance and boldness. He did not have a specific plan for his visit with Gabe. He wanted to allow him the liberty to say what was on his heart. As he welcomed him coming up the front steps, the two men shook hands and then hugged warmly. "How are you liking your sabbatical, Pastor?"

"It has been wonderful, and refreshing, and surprising," admitted Jerry.

"Surprising?"

"Yes, I was expecting to learn more about God, but I've been learning more about myself. Of course, that has led to knowing God better. Especially when I realize He really likes me, in spite of myself!"

Gabe laughed. "I know what you mean. It's like my hero, King David. When I pour out my heart to God, I find that He wants me to be real. I sense that He's most pleased when I am brutally honest. But then He always brings me to the point that I realize my attitude is pretty stinkin'."

"Yep. I'm there."

"Just the other day I was complaining about the problems and cost overruns on my new project. I was thankful that the songs had turned out so well, but the audio engineer I hired was not answering my texts on some extensive changes I wanted him to make. Up to that point he had been very responsive, but then he seemed to go dark. It was frustrating. Finally, I blew up at God and told Him that this whole project was His idea, and He was going to have to fix it. I couldn't take it anymore."

"Wow. What did He say?" Jerry said with mock horror.

"Well, nothing, of course. He let me stew for about an hour. When I finally calmed down, I began to think back on how all the pieces had come together. It had not been easy, as you know. But there was an answer for every roadblock, and more than one divine coincidence. The tracks I thought had been accidentally overwritten mysteriously appearing in a folder. Talk about a sign from heaven. I mean, some angel definitely dropped those files into the cloud."

"Yes, I remember. That was a cause for celebration."

"Well, after a few more memories of His goodness, I finally gave up and shouted, 'OK, I get it. You are God and I am not. I trust You to handle this. I'm taking my hands off. No more texts.'"

"And...?"

"What do you think? Of course, the engineer called up that evening and explained the family emergency that had taken him away for several days. I really felt bad when he said that he had been working on my project the whole time, in between hospital visits and ministering to family members. He then let me know he had just put the files in my cloud folder. Within an hour, I listened to them and let him know they were outstanding. He had done everything I had asked and more."

"So, are you giving him a bonus?" chuckled Jerry.

"Umm. Hadn't thought of that. You're kidding, but you know, I may just do it."

"Great. Now that we know Who is in charge here, let's do some praying and cast some vision. What do you say?"

"Hey, I'm ready, Pastor. I'll continue where I left off in the car."

Gabe immediately began praying boldly and confidently. He literally brought heaven down to earth as he prayed for a fresh new anointing in the worship ministry. Jerry saw that Gabe had been soaking in God's presence and was flowing in the very anointing he was praying for. Jerry joined in with complementary and equally fervent prayer. The two men went back and forth for half an hour, building on each other's words of thanksgiving, praise, confession, faith-filled petition, and more thanksgiving for the answers.

As they began to wind down with a few minutes of individual silent prayer, Jerry finally opened his eyes and said, "Gabe, that was powerful. You are truly a worshipper and a man after God's own heart. Thank you for taking us into heavenly realms. I feel so refreshed."

Gabe was a bit surprised at Jerry's effusive praise. He had never said anything like that before. Gabe tried, but could not hold back a sheepish grin. He managed to get out a single "Thanks."

Jerry recognized Gabe's discomfort and used the moment to share briefly some of the personal interaction he had with Mark the day before. He admitted that it had been uncomfortable for him, but that he had felt a huge relief when he just let it go and was able to express his feelings with Mark. He said that he didn't mean to make Gabe uncomfortable with his words of praise, and he certainly wasn't trying to flatter him. It was just the truth, and Gabe needed to hear it as much as Jerry needed to say it.

Gabe was still trying to process this simple transaction. "Pastor, I really appreciate your words. I guess I don't get much affirmation, except from my wife. I never got much from my father. Sounds like you and Mark agreed that this is all too common."

"Yes, it is, even in the ministry. I honestly didn't realize I haven't been affirming you. Maybe I thought the thought, but didn't verbalize it as I should have been doing. I guess we guys are good at banter, but we don't get around to saying out loud the things that really matter. Maybe I was impacted more than I thought yesterday. It just seemed the most natural thing to want to recognize the godliness that I see in you. I'll try not to do it too often, though. Wouldn't want anyone to think I'm getting soft."

Gabe laughed, reached out his hand to Jerry, looked him squarely in the eye as they shook, and said, "Pastor, I respect you, and I love you. This is just the boost I needed. You have confirmed that God loves me. I really needed to hear those words."

"OK, let's stay in this atmosphere and talk about your ministry. What are you hearing from the Holy Spirit, and what are you wanting to accomplish this next year?"

The men spent the next three hours discussing all aspects of the worship and music ministry. Gabe presented a number of ideas for new programs that would involve releasing worship and praise teams in several areas of the church and as "missionaries" to the community. Jerry was humbled that this young man of God was so excited and energized and wanted to serve others and see them grow in their God-given gifts. Jerry caught the same spirit and decided that he would have the same mission with the others who were coming to see him in the next few days. Rather than look for how they could fulfill his vision for the church, he decided to release them to fulfill the gifts and dreams God had already placed in their hearts. He was sure that God would work all of these together for the benefit of the local church and for the church of Christ. After all, who was he to try to orchestrate how God's plan should be fulfilled? Wasn't God able to do that through everyone being led by the Holy Spirit? They certainly didn't have to be led all the time by Jerry. He decided that his role was to be a pastor and teacher. Let the others do what they are called to do, and let God put it all together for His glory.

What Jerry didn't realize was that in the process of releasing his staff to pursue their God-given talents, he was also releasing them to return his love and faith in them, that is, in the Christ in them. And they would in turn want to serve him, and help him be the best pastor and teacher he could be. They would also want to help one another be successful. But the definition of success was now to listen to God's heart, and then work hard to bring Him joy by loving and serving one another, as He commanded them to.

Jerry would later realize that these seeds of trust in his people would bear fruit many times beyond what he could have hoped or imagined had he first tried to determine their goals or methods of achieving them. He felt led to establish a few core values for the church and then ask the staff to embody those in their efforts and programs, which they were more than happy to do. It gave everyone a sense of common purpose and a common language.

For example, with Tom and Mary Oberlin the following day, Jerry validated their dreams of a consistent children's and youth program that for each age level would identify ways in which the fruits of the spirit could be taught and modeled. Mary was aware of a curriculum for children that would assist with this vision, and Tom was eager to extend the concept with youth. It would provide a clear structure for teachers and team leaders who could then find ways to embody the fruit in examples from their own lives.

Tom even extended the idea to include goals at key points. For example, at the end of upper elementary, children should be able to have a clear understanding of the basic Bible stories, characters, and New Testament doctrines and be able to tell them to someone else. At the end of junior high they should be able to understand and explain the gifts and ministries that believers can expect to have and be given opportunities to experience them in a variety of ways. Finally, by the end of high school they should both be able to identify the particular gifts and ministries they are called to, and the purpose they believe God has for them in their life.

Jerry sat back in wonder at their creativity and passion for young people. He knew that this would go over extremely well with the adults and would result in a legacy of stability, while allowing each generation of students and teachers to bring their own creativity to illustrating the simple, but eternal principles.

Jerry began to get ideas for sermon series and men's and women's programs that would complement the children and youth curriculum. He realized that this organic approach to developing the church's programs was much better than trying to direct it from the top down. He was beginning to realize that his role was to nudge a little here and there to ensure faithfulness to the scriptures, support of the church's core values, and meeting community needs. The mayor of their city, for example, was promoting regional food banks, which Jerry gently suggested that the children and youth might want to consider in some of their efforts. That sparked all sorts of ideas with Tom and Mary, and would ultimately create a reputation for service in the community that would attract many unchurched families.

# 8

## George and Bob

Jerry's sessions later in the week with George James and Bob Newcomb were full of surprises. George had just come from some tense business meetings and at first seemed a bit distracted. It appeared that he hadn't thought too much about the session, so Jerry instead asked George about his business and what he was dealing with currently. As George began to describe the difficult situation and seemingly complex decisions that he needed to make in the next few days, Jerry realized the stress he was under. He offered to pray. Rather than a general prayer for wisdom laced with scriptures, Jerry found himself pausing regularly to hear from the Holy Spirit and then simply, but boldly, praying what he heard. He was astounded at the personal details and insight into George's life and business that were revealed. He almost skipped some thoughts, afraid they were too specific or far-fetched. But those turned out to be the most meaningful to George.

At the end of the prayer, George said, "Pastor, what just happened? I came here to hear from you and support your vision for the church. Now you have turned everything upside down and blessed me in ways you can't imagine. I have so many ideas now about not just solving my dilemma, but how it can work for the good of all the parties involved. I can't believe it."

"George, the Lord has been showing and teaching me so much the past few days. I am learning to seek Him and hear His heart for others. I knew before you arrived that I was to listen to what was really going on with you, and then give you words from the throne of heaven, even if they seemed odd. It was tough in some spots, but that's what I tried to do. I am blessed that God used me in some small way to encourage you."

"OK, I get it. Now I'm really pumped. Let me return the blessing and hear your heart for the ministry, your family, and yourself. In whatever order you want."

Jerry laughed and took George by the shoulder. "Let's get some iced tea, my friend, and sit on the porch. I've got a lot to say, and I want us to be comfortable."

Jerry unburdened his heart, just as George had asked. He shocked George once again by asking him a very uncharacteristic question. "George, you have known me for a long time and seen me at my best and at my worst. I want you to be really honest. I know that I have blind spots about my own character and how I interact with others, especially my staff and my family. I mean it, think and honestly tell me, what is one thing I can do to eliminate a character flaw that is hurting the ministry? Then, what is one thing I can do to improve how I relate to my staff? And finally, what is one way I can treat my family better?"

"Wow, you don't mess around with harmless chatter, do you? Well, since you asked for it, where do I start?"

George's smile turned serious, and then he prayed out loud for wisdom and just the right words to speak. He then spent several minutes in silence, listening to the Holy Spirit. Finally, he began to discuss these uncomfortable topics with Jerry. He didn't pull any punches, but he was led to focus on a handful of specific incidents that illustrated his comments. He used humor to ease the seriousness of the discussion, and even asked Jerry what he was feeling and thinking in a couple of the situations. He also was very sketchy in his recommendations for improvement, preferring instead to clarify his perspective of Jerry's behavior in each situation and then letting Jerry jump in with thoughts on how he could have done better.

When he was finished, he asked Jerry if he could pray for him. He took the cue from Jerry and really listened again to the Holy Spirit. He then prayed the most eloquent and heart-felt blessing and impartation for leadership that Jerry had ever heard. He felt completely validated as a pastor and as a person, and incredibly challenged to appropriate the prophetic words that had obviously come directly from God. The two men embraced and spent the next few minutes talking about how faithful and good God was. They were overwhelmed at how He had met them both at their points of deepest need.

The two men spent the rest of the afternoon discussing ideas about special projects that the men's group could get involved in. George became excited as he heard Jerry's desire to see men learn to communicate with one another and with God at new levels as the two of them had just done. George suggested a weekend retreat that would provide time and opportunity for contemplation and conversation, two things that men would almost never focus on by themselves. Jerry asked George to get with a few other men to develop an agenda that would facilitate those opportunities, along with some teaching and recreation that would set the stage for meaningful interaction. They discussed several men who would be open to such ideas and who had expressed a desire to go deeper in the things of God.

George left after a simple dinner, and Jerry spent the rest of the evening in prayers of thanksgiving, praise, and intercession for his final guest the next day, Bob Newcomb. As a member of the church board and the financial expert who mentored Mark on church business issues, Bob was a critical resource and supporter for the church, but also for Jerry personally. With all that had happened so far, Jerry was eager to see how God would draw Bob and him closer together and bring forth wisdom and direction in this critical area of the ministry. Jerry could feel the Father taking pleasure in his heart-felt joy of anticipation. It was a totally new attitude for Jerry. Accounting and finances were not his areas of expertise, to say the least, and he would normally be worried about showing Bob that he was not knowledgeable about everything the church was doing.

Jerry's fears were allayed the next morning when Bob arrived in an unusually upbeat mood. Jerry had asked him at the last board meeting to come with some ideas on how the church could reach a stronger financial position, especially in light of the additional debt they had taken on with the building program. Jerry was not prepared for what happened next. Instead of the usual spreadsheets and PowerPoints, which was how Bob normally communicated, he just had a worn, black leather Bible with a big notebook.

"Wow! You are going hi-tech, Bob."

"Yeah, I know. I decided to ditch the tablet in keeping with the rustic setting and thinking about strategy rather than numbers. Don't go into shock, Pastor, but I prayed a lot the last few days and most of last night. I think I have some fresh, hot ideas."

"Great! Let's fry up some breakfast while you're filling me in."

Bob took on bacon duty while Jerry prepared the omelets and toast. Bob continued to talk excitedly about the verses he had been studying.

"Pastor, I found myself in Proverbs, chapter 17. Verse 3 just stuck out in bold. It says 'The refining pot is for silver and the furnace for gold, but the Lord tests the hearts.'"

"OK. Not exactly one of the most popular offering scriptures, but I'm listening. By the way, strawberry or grape jam?"

As the men sat down to enjoy their traditional breakfast, Bob presented his very non-traditional mini-teaching on church finances.

"At first, I didn't see what this had to do with finance, other than the words gold and silver. But then I realized that it has the key to individual and corporate success in all areas."

"Whoa, that's a leap, Bob. Let's hear it." He had known Bob a long time and was used to his learned discourses on the fine points of investing strategies and the latest non-profit tax rulings and accounting principles, but he rarely heard Bob expound on Bible topics, and never with such fervor.

"Well, silver and gold become valuable as they are refined. But the process is very involved and requires precision at each step to extract and concentrate the precious metals to the necessary degree of purity. It's the same when we handle money or anything valuable. If we want to

# The Organic Church

extract the most value from a situation, like an investment opportunity or the resources we have as Christians, we have to follow well-established processes. These processes often take time, have to be done in a certain order, and require an uncomfortable level of heat and fire."

"Not sure I like where this is going, Bob. Kinda early in the morning to be talking about fire and heat."

"You will like it, Pastor. Just be patient," smiled Bob.

For the next thirty minutes Bob expounded on the parallels of refining precious metals and the Lord refining, or testing, our hearts. He said that it starts with individuals, and especially leaders. If we aren't pure in heart, then we can't hope to know God's direction for ourselves, much less for others. Also, we should look forward to the period of testing, i.e., refining, by the heat of trials and even the fires of tribulation and persecution. As with gold and silver, there is often a fine line between too much and not enough heat. Too much can burn or vaporize the metal, and not enough heat will have no impact at all. We simply have to trust the recipe for refining and hold just the right temperature for just the amount of time required. We cannot shortcut the process and get the desired results. And we have to mix in the right substances, even acids that would seem to be toxic and dangerous.

Jerry was fascinated at Bob's intensity and depth of understanding of this uncomfortable teaching that pastors typically avoid. He tried to inject humor a couple of times, but it was clear that Bob was leading up to something significant. He ask him point blank, "So, how do you see this principle applying to me and the church?"

"I'm getting there, Pastor. I'm not trying to imply that you are not where you should be or that you are doing anything without pure motives."

"Hold it. Of course I am not pure, at least not most of the time. I know I need refining. That's exactly why I am here, talking to you, to others I respect, and to God. So let's be real. I can take it. I don't want to be flattered. I want to be everything God wants me to be, and I am willing to hear hard things and do hard things. Press on."

"OK, Pastor, but you understand this is hard for me to say, because I'm in the same boat. I am hearing truths that are convicting me as well, and I hesitate to say things that I haven't been able to put fully into practice. But I know I am supposed to bring them up to you. Maybe together we can figure out what they mean and how we can use them for ourselves and for the church corporately."

"Exactly, Bob. So continue. After all I've been through the past few days, you have my full attention!"

"Well, it's almost too simple. I believe that the keys to all of this are rest and timing."

"Wow. I was expecting proactive words like courage and boldness in the face of opposition. Not passivity."

"Yeah, surprised me, too. But I believe that being able to rest and wait on God's timing shows the ultimate level of trust. And that is what faith, the kind that pleases Him, is all about."

"Yes, I get it, Bob. That is so true."

"One final observation, Pastor. And this goes to your point. When the time is ripe for action, then we must listen very carefully and do only what we hear the Holy Spirit saying, nothing more, nothing less, just as Jesus did every day. Not sure how we can do that with all the distractions and emergencies we face, but that's what I know we are supposed to strive for."

"Are you done?"

"Yep, I got nothing else. That's already way over my ability to handle it."

"Mine, too, Bob, but I think I see a way out. And I think I see how this moves from the personal to the corporate."

"Really? That's awesome. How?"

"Well, it's just forming in my mind. Let's see if the fish are biting this morning, and maybe letting this truth rest for a bit will give us deeper understanding. What do you say?"

"Hey, I'm game. No pun intended, Pastor."

"None taken," said Jerry, suppressing a smile.

The two men kept busy the rest of the morning with a school of sand bass just off the point, a few minutes boat ride from the cabin's dock. As they returned with enough filets for a late lunch and for several additional sabbatical meals, they resumed their discussion of Proverbs 17:3.

"So, Pastor, I think the mess of fish was a sign that we are on to something. You know, like casting the net on the other side."

Jerry smiled, thinking of the earlier conversation with Mark that alluded to the same fishing passage. The implication was not lost on him.

"Maybe more than we know, Bob. I have some thoughts on how this could happen. First, it is critical that we start with ourselves. How can we lead others where we haven't been? What does that look like? I think it means embracing every issue, every problem, and every trial as a step towards being refined. And just as you said, trusting completely in the Lord, which means being patient and actually having an attitude of rest. The way I think of that is having a knowing that He is in control—not just head knowledge, but a real gut-level heart knowing. I'm thinking that this would come from rejecting any negative thoughts of fear or worry about what might go wrong, focusing on a past example of seeing Him work things out for the good, and then resting in that expectation for this situation. Maybe even smiling inwardly and saying to Him, 'I can't wait to see how You do it this time!'

"I think that is the key to resting in the moment. We are to be confident based on the Word and on past experiences of trusting in that Word. It's like when the utility company trimmed our trees along the back easement. I see now how God used that to show others how to handle circumstances beyond their control and to not lose their witness in front of those who are watching us. I'm just sorry that at the time I didn't see it clearly as a test. I stumbled through it, but not necessarily with the best motive. That, however, is my goal. I think that will happen as I recognize incidents like that as opportunities rather than as obstacles. What do you think?"

"Yes, Pastor, absolutely. That is a great way to think about it. Not easy to do, but easy to remember, at least. I know when I am working on the church's finances, it is so easy to slip into the worry/what if mode. I guess the way to avoid that is to pray something like 'Lord, this is a great opportunity to see Your faithfulness. What would You have us learn in this situation? And what should our response be?' Sometimes I go there, but more often I get caught up in worrying about who's to blame, where to cut expenses, or how to be more effective in fund-raising. I completely lose sight of the bigger picture about finances just being a tool, and that the purity of our hearts is the real measure of success."

"Yes, Bob, and I think you are beginning to touch on how this affects us corporately. It's my job and yours, in our roles as stewards of God's people and resources, to keep that bigger picture in mind at all times. But more than that, as we get good at these tests, this refining process, we need to communicate that to the people so they see it working at both personal and corporate levels. Just like they need to see it work for themselves, their family, with friends, or in their job. You mentioned this when you first came in today as a key to success in church finances. What are you thinking about that?"

"You know, I'm not so sure now. Initially I was thinking in general terms that we just need to roll our personal and corporate financial concerns on the Lord and not get into fear or worry. But the more we talk, I think each area of our lives may have tests and a refining process that we need to understand. Finances is one of those areas, probably the most obvious indicator of our spiritual health. So let's pray about that right now.

"Lord, we want to be good stewards. Help us to understand how to navigate the financial tests that we all go through, both personally and as a church. If there are principles or processes that will help us, we want to hear them from You. Or from people You have ordained for this purpose. There, let's just meditate a few minutes and wait on the Holy Spirit."

After a couple of minutes, Jerry said, "You know, Bob, I'm really feeling that the key to church finances is to get our personal finances in order. If we can do that as individuals, as pastors, as staff, and as church members, I think that will change the atmosphere. I think it's a combination of having a pure heart, which would be that of a generous, cheerful giver, but also a prudent spirit that is careful to use our God-given resources wisely.

"As far as principles, there are lots of classes we could offer to help our people in this area. We had one a few years ago, but I need to restart it and really encourage that as a means for both helping individuals and the church. A class will give people the practical principles, but then I need to prepare the church for the testing process. That's what your scripture verse is saying. Along the way to financial success, there will be a lot of temptations and trials, right?"

"Of course. The devil is very good at discouraging us in lots of ways."

"Exactly. If we can see those tests as being like the fire or acid in the precious metal refining process, then we can see that the process is working as expected. If we bypass those steps, you will still have the metal, but it will be tainted with impurities and will not be as beautiful or as valuable."

"Yes, Pastor, I see where you are going. You could have a sermon series that would expose the devil's devices and then show how God uses the very thing that looks harmful to make the refining process more effective. It will be easy to apply that to finances, but it also applies to other areas of our lives."

"Yep. That's it, Bob. I have done several sermons on giving, but I haven't really laid it out in this way. I'm excited to see how this unfolds. I think it could be the key to releasing our folks from a scarcity mentality. Our God wants us to know how to live gracefully with lack, as Paul did. But He also wants us to have our needs met and be able to give generously to others. We can do it as we learn to turn Satan's trials and temptations into purifying tests. My job is to identify the questions on that 'test' and then help our people prepare for it. It won't work to cram the night before, because we don't know when they are coming. We just have to be ready and able to discern the test for what it is and what it can be."

"Pastor, I think that is right on. Let me know what I can do to help you prepare. Maybe we can visit more about this and I can suggest some practical tests and preparation."

"That's great Bob. Let's do it. I think that will be one of the first sermon series what I get back."

"Yes, everyone is already eager to see you back. The guest speakers have been good, but we want to hear from you. We know you will have a fresh word for us and that you will back it up with action."

"That's nice of you to say. I can't wait to get back. I have so many things already that I want to share. It's good, though, that I have another week to soak on these things and develop them into messages. I am also seeing how I can speak into some of our ministries and programs so that we are not just hearing principles on Sunday, but that we are putting them into practice in other ways.

"Well, Bob, it's been great having you here. You are the last of my visitors, but certainly not the least. I have learned some amazing things. I pray that the Holy Spirit will be with you and guide you as you continue to help guide our church toward financial blessing and security."

"Thank you, Pastor, and may God richly bless the rest of your sabbatical. I am excited to see what all He is doing through you!"

As Bob made his way back to his truck, Jerry got on his knees and began to offer thanks to God for orchestrating the past few days' visits. He was in awe at the completely different direction each of these visits had taken, and at the miraculous results that were changing his heart forever. He was not only no longer afraid of the "R" word, but he eagerly looked forward to revival. Now he understood that he had no way of knowing what it would look like, what form it would take, or how or when it would come about. He just knew that an infinitely creative God would work all things together for His precious people who were the called according to His purpose. And further, that he was looking forward with joy to being completely surprised. He just needed to trust God to work sovereignly in each church member and bring them to the point of being ready to receive a miracle from Heaven.

# 9

## Preparation

Over the next few days, Jerry began to prepare sermon outlines and do research for some of the early series he was feeling led to preach. He also realized that the visits with his key staff and friends had been about changing character and deepening intimacy with God and others. He needed to continue on this journey, while communicating to his staff and congregation what he was learning and experiencing. He must simply trust God to use him, no matter how unqualified he might feel.

Jerry felt that to do this, he should step up his sermon preparation to a whole new level. While his research would involve the same study tools and topical searches, once he was ready to write, he would abandon his standard procedure for first developing a simple outline with key principles, Biblical illustrations, and personal applications. Instead, he would take an approach similar to receiving a prophetic word for himself or someone else. He typically would have a quiet time of worship and prayer, followed by a request to hear directly from the Holy Spirit. Then he would write down the words he was hearing without doubt or hesitation. In these situations, he had no idea what was coming, so it was fairly easy to step out in faith and just start writing. He found that the less he thought about it, the easier it was to start and the more readily the words flowed. He was always amazed at how simple and accurate the resulting few sentences or paragraphs were. He had never thought to try that on a longer writing exercise, like a sermon. He had always assumed, as he was taught in Bible school, that he needed to follow a particular form to ensure clarity of thought. But out of obedience, and wanting to trust God in new and exciting ways, he decided that he would step out with confidence.

He tried it on one outline and was surprised at how the process worked. At first it was uncomfortable not knowing what the next word, much less the next thought, was going to be. However, as he kept at it faithfully, the Holy Spirit was likewise faithful to give him the words and thoughts to record. Sometimes it was word for word, as with his personal prophetic writings. Then he might get a thought and feel led to put it into his own words, drawing on a specific teaching or incident from the past. He found that he was able to put together a full sermon text in just a few hours. Even more surprising were the unusual insights and passages that came to mind as the Holy Spirit guided his thoughts.

After his first quick draft, he was able to step back and look at the result as a whole and see additional ways to illustrate and structure the sermon. Finally, he decided to try the Charles Spurgeon technique that he had learned in his research on revivals. He made a keyword outline of his text to be used when delivering the sermon. On his first practice session, he found that much of what he had written flowed naturally, but he was also open to new thoughts. It was a liberating experience to be able to do preparation under the guidance of the Holy Spirit and then try to deliver it in a fresh way.

In his joy at learning something new about an area he thought he had mastered, Jerry looked back on the interactions he had experienced with his staff and friends the past few days. He realized that, while he had many good relationships, he didn't have many really close friends. He didn't have many people with whom he could share his deepest needs or secrets as he had begun to do in these recent visits. This was the cry of his heart, to develop more meaningful relationships with others and with God. How can you say you love God if you don't love others—but that can be extended to say how can you go deeper with God if you don't go deeper with people? So how would he do that? Should it be in the context of his role as leader of the men's ministry? Or should he seek out specific men in his church or elsewhere and make individual efforts?

As he prayed about it, the Holy Spirit gave him a strategy. He already had a small group of leaders in the men's group that he would like to go deeper with, both individually and as a group. He also wanted to see them go deeper with one another. He decided to take them through a highly interactive but structured program that would create opportunities for sharing their life stories. His hope was that it would encourage them to reveal deep needs and pray for those needs to be met. He saw that this would naturally lead to doing life with them individually and with their families. He was ready to experience more of the Father's love, and he felt that Godward love is connected to love for people in the nitty gritty details of life.

The quest for revival was going to come through honest relationships more so than through finding the right teaching or right formula for getting prayers answered. After all, it's what Jesus did when He experienced everyday life. He had a regular job, was baptized by John, and then chose twelve men to demonstrate love to and through in daily ministry for three years.

During these final days of his sabbatical, Jerry realized that he was no longer afraid of "revival." Rather than bringing up the normal baggage of issues and hype, the word began to have an entirely different connotation for him. He had been developing a taste, even a thirst, for deeper intimacy with others and with God. He now saw that "revival" was just a matter of realizing a deeper level of experiencing everyday life. It was truly "re-living" the way God intended us to live in the first place—in abandonment and communion with Him and with one another.

Jerry realized there was no need, or expectation, of emotional, super-spiritual feelings or wild services. It was all about transforming his own heart to turn toward God first, and then toward others in genuine humility. Then, and only then, would God truly work in his life and touch others through him. There was nothing for him to do, no sermon series to preach, no evangelist to bring in, and no miracles of healing to pray down. It was just a matter of turning his heart and mind. Isn't that what "repentance" really means? It is turning your soul from its current self-centered path to one of absolute dependence on God and service to others through His grace.

As Jerry began to understand the magnitude of this revelation, a supernatural peace settled over him. He felt no anxiety about having to perform or make anything happen. He just had to focus on being real with God and being real in his interactions with his wife, his family, and his people.

After dwelling on the idea of repentance and its many facets, Jerry realized that it is simply the message of the cross. It started with John the Baptist's call for repentance, which Jesus reiterated and deepened to apply even to a person's thought life and attitudes. Then, in the ultimate confirmation, He provided the means by which we can repent and actually have the power to overcome the lure of sin. That power comes not from our own will, but from God's grace. And that grace took the form of Jesus paying the penalty for sin once and for all, demonstrating His power over it, and giving us the benefits of that power through remembering His sacrifice and going forward with the Holy Spirit to lead us into all truth and righteousness.

The Crucifixion was the ultimate sacrifice that gives us the ultimate resource to overcome our flesh and the devil's temptations. It all came from Calvary, the message of the cross. Jerry remembered the teaching that some denominations leave Jesus on the cross and that we should focus instead on the resurrection. But Jerry now knew that we must always behold that sacrificial cross as well. We must apply that divine lesson of grace that was poured out in such a heart-piercing but infinitely loving way.

As Jerry thought about old sermons, hymns, books, and movie scenes on the Crucifixion, the agony of the Father came flooding over him. Jerry realized that Jesus was drinking the cup of God's wrath. The Father's righteous fury at sin was poured out on His only Son who experienced total rejection and separation, the essence of Hell itself. How could the innocent, sinless One have to go through such punishment and such despair, all because of our sins?

But then it was over, and through that one instance of obedience, Jesus provided a way for us to experience eternal joy and abundant life. We simply repent, ask the Father to forgive us, and accept by faith that we can overcome evil through the grace of the cross. "It is finished" in God's sight. He likewise gives us by grace to understand His will for us every minute of every day. We just need to listen and to step out in faith, as Jesus did for our example.

The simplicity and the magnitude of the cross once again amazed Jerry. As he thought about it, though, he could not remember the last time he preached a sermon on the full message of the cross with bold clarity. He touched on it during the Easter season, of course, but not regularly the rest of the year. He resolved to base every sermon theme on this foundation, on the rock Christ Jesus, His death and resurrection, and the Holy Spirit power that we have available, because he recognized that the cross is the heart of Christianity and the key to our daily success in overcoming this world. The call to action would always involve repentance and turning our hearts back to the Father in gratefulness for His grace and mercy. Only then can we be free from the traps of the enemy, the fear of man, and our own insecurity and shame.

But there was one more thing he had to do. He knew that historic revivals, and even Jesus' ministry, were all birthed and sustained with intense and continual prayer. This was not just on the part of the main preacher, but it permeated the entire body of worshippers. It was regularly practiced in small groups and paved the way for all services. Jerry committed to making prayer a priority and establishing it as a discipline. He even decided to hire a part-time prayer pastor who would teach on all types of prayer, from soaking, personal devotional prayer, to intense intercession for others, to full blown spiritual warfare, including deliverance from demonic oppression.

But more than teach, this pastor would demonstrate, as Jesus did throughout His ministry on earth, that prayer is the key to healing of every kind, for every believer. We must hear in prayer what the Father is wanting to do, and then step out in obedience to see Him perform His will every day. To seal his commitment to prayer, Jerry spent the last day of the sabbatical fasting and praying for the prayer ministry, and specifically for a prayer pastor. He was confident that God would bring the perfect person across his path, and that he would receive a supernatural confirmation.

Finally, on the last day of his time at the cabin, Jerry reviewed his journal of the past few weeks. He felt led to add a prophetic entry that flowed from his heart, as he believed he was being led by the Holy Spirit. He wrote, "God, You are the Almighty, the Everlasting One, the Beginning and the End. I love You and adore You. I give You these past two weeks. I lay down any expectations of what I think may happen from this point on. Let Your perfect will be done in my life. I give You my wife, my children, my church staff and congregation. They are not mine at all, but Yours. I am just Your steward of them for a short time. These are Your precious saints whom You have entrusted to me. How unworthy and humbled I am to watch over their souls. And yet I know that no man can pluck them from Your hand. You have secured them forever. And You have given me the unspeakable privilege of serving them for a few years. May my heart always be toward You and toward them. Keep me from the temptation to think myself in any way superior, or in any way responsible for their eternal destiny. I can rest freely in knowing that You love them more than I ever will. God, do not allow me to hurt them in any lasting way. I know I will do things that will hurt them, sometimes with good intentions. Please get my attention in those situations, and give me the grace to see and admit my failings, to repent and ask forgiveness, and to learn from my sin. God, let me be an example of a life lived at the foot of the Cross, always beholding Your sacrifice that I might be made whole and help others become whole. May we all grow together in grace and truth, and may we learn what revival of our souls is all about."

As Jerry was packing up his gear and loading the car, he thought back on the two weeks of sabbatical. He had heard God's voice more clearly than ever before, but he also had drawn closer to key staff and friends than ever before. This confirmed his understanding that relationship with God and relationships with his fellow men were divinely interrelated.

While driving home, he committed to being the most loving father and husband, the most compassionate friend, and the most understanding boss and pastor that he could possibly be. This was his deepest desire and his greatest prayer. He sensed the Father's approval and love as he approached his neighborhood. He knew that he was in the center of God's will.

# 10

## Back Home

"Hey, Dad!" shouted Steve as he ran to meet Jerry at the driveway. He opened the car door for his father and wrapped his arms around his waist. "I missed you so much!"

"I missed you too, Steve. I think you've grown an inch or two. Help me inside with my bags, and I want to hear all about your summer since our camping trip."

"You bet. Bring any fish back? I'm hungry for more fried catfish."

"Of course. Just for you. I've got enough for 3 or 4 meals, or maybe a fish fry for some friends."

"Hey, that's a good idea! Let's have some families over for a welcome home fish fry. I'm on it."

"OK. Let's tell Mom. She can help you plan it. I would really appreciate it. I missed everyone."

Donna met them at the door and gave Jerry a big kiss. "Mom, please!" said Don, as he poked his head around the door. "Let me hug him, too."

"And me," chimed in Stephanie. "Hi Dad. It's good to have you home. It's been pretty boring around here without you. Did you get lots done at the cabin?"

"You mean besides the boatload of fish I caught?" As she rolled her eyes, Jerry continued, "You wouldn't believe all of the great ideas I got and all of the lessons I learned. I'll try to get my thoughts together and share them over dinner tonight. In the meantime, I want to hear what all has happened around here the past two weeks. Let's go from youngest to oldest."

As Steve began to talk rapidly and excitedly about his summer adventures, Jerry found that he had a new capacity to focus on what Steve was saying. He felt his youngest son's energy and desire for his attention and love. He stopped him a number of times to ask questions and probe for more details. He found himself even asking things like, "How did that make you feel?" and "I'll bet that made you proud!" Steve was beaming as he and his Dad carried on a long conversation in front of the whole family. He was loving the attention that he so often didn't feel he got as the youngest. He knew that some people, especially his brother and sister, were annoyed at his talkative and sometimes crazy behavior. But in this moment his Dad was listening to him, and that made him feel good.

As Steve wound down, Jerry looked at Don and asked how his baseball team was doing. Don didn't say much, but his dad asked questions about the different pitchers that Don caught for. As Don warmed up, he realized that his dad was really interested and had been paying close attention to his team's season. So he gave him blow by blow details of the most important game against their main rival. When he said that he made the winning out by catching a tough foul ball, Jerry grabbed him by the shoulders, looked into his eyes, and said, "Son, I am so proud of you. Way to go. I wish I had been there. I'm going to try to make up for it by coming to more of your games."

"That would be great, Dad. I'd really like that."

By the time Jerry was well into a similarly intimate conversation with Stephanie about her recent activities, Donna was sure that something big had happened to her husband. She had never seen him be so intentional with each of the children, especially in a group setting. At first she thought it was just that he missed them and was trying to catch up on their activities. But as she saw the warmth and interest he showed by asking specific questions and by looking into their eyes with obvious pride, she realized that a significant shift had occurred, and it was already beginning to transform their family. Had her prayers for Jerry and the family been answered?

Her thoughts were suddenly interrupted with Jerry's words directed at her. "And what about my darling wife? You have gotten more beautiful than ever! I think being away from me has done you some good. But don't get used to it. So what have you been doing besides being an exceptional mother, cook, chauffeur, and everything else?"

As Donna was filling in the kids' stories and mentioning things that had happened to others in their close circle of friends and church members, she was intrigued by her husband's smile and what she imagined to be a twinkle in his eyes. While she was still questioning whether Jerry had a clue about how he had taken her for granted during the family vacation, and many times before, something stirred in her to want to know this man even deeper and to experience what had so obviously influenced his very soul these past weeks. His questions for her showed a loving concern for her emotional state. It was not at all concern for having to bear additional responsibility in his absence, but rather wanting to know how she had grown and learned from the experience.

After the children were in their rooms, Jerry and Donna talked into the early morning hours. They both had full hearts and were eager to share thoughts that had been forming during the sabbatical. Donna had learned a lot about herself and her relationship to her children. Without Jerry's daily influence she developed a more balanced role. She was a natural nurturer and knew that she tended to overdo it, especially with Steve. She had always protected him, being the youngest, but even more so when his learning difference was diagnosed.

She unconsciously depended on Jerry to provide the balance of challenging and disciplining Steve, but in his absence, she realized that she also needed to play that role. She found it difficult at first, sensing that Steve felt annoyed and a little betrayed when his advocate and defender also became his disciplinarian. The big "aha!" for her was when she sat down with him one evening and discussed the situation frankly. She told him how uncomfortable it made her feel, but that she was doing it because she loved him so much. Steve had trouble processing her train of thought, but when he saw how sincere his mother was and that her love for him was so very deep, he decided that he could trust her, even though he didn't fully understand why she had to change her behavior towards him.

As Donna was explaining all of this to Jerry, he marveled at her wisdom and the positive change it had already made in their son. She had turned what could have been a negative, confrontational situation into an opportunity for growth in both Steve and herself. Donna confided that she hadn't thought it was going to work out this way. At the time, it seemed to be a huge risk for her to take. She prayed and felt an unusual peace about taking this uncharacteristic step. She said that if her husband was going to have a time of reflection and commitment to change, perhaps she could use everyday circumstances to see God work in her life and in her family. She had to admit that she was a bit shocked at how things had turned out so well. It had given her hope that she could continue to learn and grow by moving toward such "opportunities," or to be more frank, "challenges," rather than dreading them.

Jerry had to chuckle, not at his wife's self-deprecating humor, but at how clever God was. Jerry had prayed that Donna would have strength and courage while he was away, but he never expected Him to use what should have been a difficult period for her to be a blessing instead. He realized that he was not chuckling so much at God, as at his own disbelief and lack of understanding of how good God really is. Jerry shared this insight with Donna, and then he continued sharing many of the others that had come from his sabbatical. Finally, when neither could keep from yawning, they snuggled together in bed and quickly fell asleep after a lingering goodnight kiss.

# 11

## Back in the Office

Jerry knew that his first day back in the office would be tough, but he was soon overwhelmed at how much had stacked up in his absence. He appreciated that the staff had left him alone during the sabbatical, but they had piled up many issues and decisions for his return. Those who had visited him at the cabin made a pact that they would not bother him with day-to-day news or problems, and instead focus on personal and longer term issues. The main area he had to deal with was finances. The offerings had remained normal in his absence, but the bank had called about the loan made during the building program that ended earlier in the year. Mark was trying to manage the issue, but he was frustrated. He met with Jerry the first morning he was back.

"Pastor Jerry, I am so sorry to have to bring this to you, but it has finally gone past my ability to handle. I even brought Bob in on this, but he said only you can take care of it."

"OK, Mark, calm down and start from the beginning."

"Well, you remember when we took out the temporary construction loan with the understanding that the bank would set the permanent loan rate to vary with prime plus 1%?"

"Sure. It was discussed at length with the board. They, including Bob, thought it was a very good deal. Why, what happened?"

"You won't believe it, but now they, including the president, say that the prime rate they were referring to is for their AA customers, and is not tied to the Fed's rate as we were led to believe."

"What? Are you serious? I'm sure that is what the agreement said. Did we miss something?"

"Unfortunately, we didn't pin down the definition in exactly those words. But everyone I talked to remembers that we were a bit skeptical at the great rate and asked me to double check with the loan officer, which I did. It was very clear in my mind that he was referring to the Federal Reserve's Prime rate."

"Yes, I remember that. It was one of the reasons we went with them rather than our regular bank."

"Well, now the loan officer and the president are adamant that the wording is very clear and that the rate is actually about 1.5% higher than we thought. That is almost 20% more interest than what we were expecting."

"OK. I will handle this personally with the bank. Get me the documents, the board meeting minutes, and emails from Bob and the others regarding their recollections."

After sensing the rising anger, Jerry felt a caution and told Mark, "Second thought, hold off on approaching the board members. Let me think about this and how I want to deal with the bank."

"Of course, Pastor. Whatever you say. Personally, I think the bank is taking advantage of us. The more I think about it, the loan officer was very reluctant to change their 'attorney-approved language' and made me feel like I wasn't up on the latest loan procedures. He was very smooth about ensuring that we were getting a sweetheart rate that was the best we could get anywhere. He was right about that, with the assumptions we made that he seemed to be confirming."

"Mark, I guarantee I will give this the highest priority."

Jerry had two more appointments before lunch with George James, but his mind was hardly able to absorb anything else. After they were over, he debated with himself about mentioning the bank loan to George. But then he remembered their discussion at the cabin about being real with one another. So he resolved to not put on his normal "God works all things for good" smiley face and instead allow George to hear about his feelings of pain and betrayal.

"Hey, Pastor Jerry," said George cheerfully, assuming they would pick up where they left off at the cabin, on a spiritual high. "How is it coming down off the mountain—cabin, that is?" George's playful opening did not have the expected response.

"Well, George, it has been a quick descent. Right into the pit."

"Oops! I guess I'm sorry I asked. I figured you would still be floating in the clouds. Did something happen back at the ranch?"

"Yes, you could say that. It has been a brutal morning." After Jerry filled George in on the gist of the issue, he got right to the point with unaccustomed transparency. "George, I don't think I've ever had such spiritual whiplash. I had the most amazing, intimate sessions with God, with staff members, with old friends, and finally last night at home with my kids and wife. Then I get blindsided this morning with what sure looks to be premeditated betrayal by our banker. I just am having a hard time squaring all of this. I mean, we had a great relationship with them during the building program and the construction. Most of those we worked with are church goers and seemed to be sincere in wanting to help us. I'm flabbergasted at their insistence on sticking to the letter of the agreement, when it was clearly, at least in our minds, not what we were encouraged to believe it was. I am so disappointed. I know we could easily have asked for more explicit language, and we certainly will next time, but, well, I've said enough. You are seeing the real Jerry at his worst. I am actually beginning to get angry, no, mad about the situation. Especially at the loan officer and the bank president."

"Pastor, I know this won't help much, but I've negotiated a lot of contracts in my long career, and I wish I could say I thought of everything every time. Sometimes things just slip through. I agree that the bank's attitude stinks. It sure sounds like an intentional deception. So what are your plans? Are you going to confront them?"

"Of course, I have to. You are the only person, besides Mark, that I am talking to about this before I go to the president. I wanted to hear from you first, though. I know you will have godly advice that I am probably not in a position to see on my own. Frankly, if it were up to me the way I feel now, I believe I would ask him to step out into the alley and face me like a man. Then I would get the slickest lawyer I could find to sue his bank, his loan officer, and him personally for misrepresentation and fraud!"

"Well, Pastor, after our last encounter, I knew that I should be prepared for this lunch. I had no idea what was going on, but I did spend some time this morning with the Lord about you. I almost never have this happen, but I had a clear picture, or more like a video, of you in my mind. You were wearing the same clothes you had at the lake cabin, and you were out in the boat, with glassy smooth water.

"You had just landed a nice bass, when a cloud appeared from nowhere and the wind began to blow. I found myself praying out loud for your safety as the waves were coming over the boat's bow while you slowly made your way back to the dock. You had trouble tying up, dropped your tackle, and the stringer of fish into the water as you fell stepping onto the dock. You were exhausted, hurt, and fought back the tears.

"Then I heard a voice say, 'Let it out, Jerry, just let it out.' You fell to your knees on the dock and began to weep—no, sob uncontrollably. I wanted to be embarrassed for you, but I realized that this was something you had to go through. And even with the loss, you would be stronger. As you got up and made your way up to the dry cabin, your face began to change. You went from tears and frustration to peace and even a quiet, determined, joy. I will never forget the look on your face as you opened the cabin door. Like a man who had been tested and had been found worthy of more authority.

"Well, I guess you would call that an anti-fish tale! But seriously, Pastor, I knew something important had happened and that I was to tell you about this, vision, I suppose you would call it. I can still see it as clearly as if it were on that screen over there. And I still feel the compassion and yet confidence in how God would bring you through the trial. So that's my message. Fortunately, I didn't have to even think about it. God had already provided the answer, even before I knew you needed one. Well, I bet you never expected anything like that from practical old George."

Jerry sat stunned in the diner booth. He was grateful they had some privacy, because he wasn't sure if he was going to laugh and shout or break down and cry. His emotions were swirling almost palpably in his chest and gut. Finally, he stared straight at George and said, "Old friend, you have just pulled me out of the miry clay. I mean, I was sinking and going deeper the harder I tried to figure a way out. I hate to think what I would have said and done when I met with the bank tomorrow. I think I would have undone everything I gained on my sabbatical, and more. You have saved me, my family, and this church from a major embarrassment. No, not just an embarrassment, a major setback in our growth. I am so glad you were faithful to pray this morning, that you were spiritually attuned to what God is saying, and that you were bold enough, and loved me enough, to tell it like you heard and saw it. George, I think I am going to buy your lunch. Shoot, maybe even dinner sometime."

"Right, Pastor. That'll be the day. I tell you what, I would pay anything to be used by God like that again. It's never happened before, but you know, maybe I need to ask and expect more of that kind of revelation. The Holy Spirit is supposed to guide us and show us things to come, right?"

"You are so right on. If nothing else happened on my sabbatical, the two of us being able to hear from God in the midst of a terrible trial is worth every bit of the time and sacrifice. Of course, as you saw in the vision, that tackle and those fish weren't recovered. I'm still going to talk to the bank about what happened and appeal for some mercy. But I won't have any expectations, and I will pray that God forgives them of any wrong motives, just as I have already forgiven them for the damage they have inflicted on me and this church. It's like the discussion Bob Newcomb and I had about testing us through the fire of circumstances and trials. I am determined to come through this with a purer heart. I may have cost the church some hard-earned money, but I am going to see it as a cheap price for becoming stronger in the Lord."

"OK, Pastor, I'm ready to eat. We have something to celebrate. I'm thinking this might even mean dessert at the end." And with a wink he added, "Especially since you are buying!"

# 12

## The Family Budget

The next few weeks, as Jerry worked back into a routine, he began to incorporate his sabbatical insights and experiences into sermons and the men's group retreat planning. There was a sweet atmosphere in the offices as the impact of the mini-sabbatical sessions with the staff yielded the fruit of peace and unity. Even the bank incident was smoothed over as a lesson in forgiving one's adversaries. While the bank didn't relent from their position, God was faithful to provide a supernatural increase in building fund contributions that almost exactly offset the unexpected interest payment increase.

Jerry's home life, however, was a different story. While the church had paid for the basics for the family vacation and Jerry's salary during the sabbatical, there were a lot of unexpected expenses over the last few weeks. A credit card payment was not made on time, and an exorbitant interest rate kicked in. Donna also had to withdraw a significant amount from their emergency fund to pay for the additional vacation items, medical and summer tutoring expenses for Steve, and unusual senior year fees for Stephanie's private Christian school. Donna was not accustomed to handling these kind of budget issues, and even though she and Jerry had agreed that this would be a good opportunity for her to have a refresher on family finances, the unexpected items had overwhelmed her.

At their monthly family budget meeting, the tension was palpable. Jerry started off with a joke about how he had been living off the land and water to keep his food expenses down, but only Steve laughed. Stephanie was the first to respond. "Dad, this sabbatical has really stressed Mom and me out. We tried to keep calm, but my school fees for graduation and the senior trip had to be paid before the first day of classes. It doesn't seem fair. They changed the rules this summer, and now our budget is all messed up."

"Stephanie, honey," said Donna, "it's not all that bad. We can reduce our beginning of school clothing and supplies costs by just waiting a month. And I will just have to ignore the letters from the other seniors asking for support for their senior missions trip expenses. After all, we have our own to take care of this year."

"But Mom, Dad, that's not right! I worked hard to save money for my portion of the trip. And all of my friends are going to feel let down if the Pastor doesn't help them with their fund raisers like you always do. They tell me every year how generous you are. It's going to be embarrassing if we don't help my friends."

"Don't worry, Sis, I've got an idea. You and your friend can hold a bake sale! You'll make tons with your chocolate sour cream cheesecake."

"Don, you are such a dork! That would be a drop in the bucket. And none of my friends know how to cook anyway. Mom, Dad, what are we going to do? You have to do something! I'm going to be the laughing-stock, especially if I have to wear the same outfits as last year. I've grown at least an inch, well maybe almost an inch."

Donna looked plaintively at Jerry, but said nothing. Jerry looked back, first with a blank expression, and then with a puzzled look and shrug of his shoulders that said he had no idea what to do.

"Honey, Stephanie is right. We have to do something. This is her senior year. It's a special time, and we have to make exceptions to this budget process. Right, kids?"

Jerry felt betrayed. Donna and he had worked for years to finally get out of debt, and were just beginning to have peace in their finances. This seemed like such a small sacrifice to stay with their program that had served them so well. Especially considering how much they had done without the past few years. The vacation and sabbatical had come as a reward from heaven for their diligence and discipline.

How could this arguing, even anger, be happening? They should be used to sucking it up by now. Did the vacation spoil them? Are they now feeling entitled to have things regardless of whether they could afford it? Were they starting back down that slippery slope they had worked so hard to get out of? These and other thoughts flooded Jerry's mind. He knew better than to give voice to them all, but he couldn't help making some comment to let everyone know his position.

"Let's think about this for a moment. Have we worked so long to fall back into old habits now and think we have to meet everyone else's expectations? If we can't afford something, we don't do it. Isn't that what we agreed to years ago? Where is all this bellyaching coming from? Aren't you grateful for our fun summer vacation and the church's generosity in giving us a sabbatical?"

Well, that set them off. Even Steve was indignant. "Dad, you may have had a great time at the cabin fishing and all, but I had to go to tutoring every day. It was awful. And it turns out, we couldn't even afford it. Now I won't get my new shoes like I always do before school starts. I'll be the only one with old raggedy sneaks that pinch my feet. It isn't fair!"

"OK," consoled Donna, "your father is under a lot of stress. He is having to adjust back to the real world, and we are going to have to cut him some slack. Let's try to be patient. I'm sure he will think of something that is not so drastic."

Sensing the irritation in her voice, Jerry shot back, "Well, I appreciate your concern, but we don't need patience. We need to stop spending money for a couple of months. We've done this before. It's as simple as that. End of story. This meeting is over. Now what's for dinner?"

The next few days in the Smith household were as chilly as the leftovers that were served three nights in a row. Donna and Jerry were barely speaking to one another, and only with strained politeness. Jerry was dumbfounded at her reaction and at the kids' stubbornness. It was such a turnabout from the supportive attitude the night before and earlier in the summer. But he wasn't going to let it get to him. He had had to be strict about the budget before, and they would see that it was for the ultimate good.

Later in the week, at the church office, Jerry was preparing for a Thanksgiving sermon series. It was a short one, just two Sundays. He had a few ideas from his sabbatical notes, but was needing to get the big picture and some memorable illustrations. It was his custom to begin with prayer, and he smiled at the first thought that popped into his head. It was the scripture, "Come into His gates with thanksgiving."

As he began to enthusiastically recite what he was thankful for, however, he realized that most of it had to do with his family. He almost without thinking was able to list many qualities he was thankful for in his children, Stephanie, Don, and Steve, and especially in his wife, Donna. He had seen so much of them during the vacation, and he quickly saw what a blessing from God they were to him. He also was reminded of the awkwardness and pain in the family the past few days. At first he felt annoyance at their reactions that caused this painful episode. But then his prayer turned to God in genuine intercession that their hurts might be healed. When he paused for a few seconds, he unexpectedly heard an inner Voice ask the question, "Why don't you talk to Donna about this?"

Jerry's first thought was to mention this to her later tonight, after he had got his initial thoughts on the sermon series written out. However, he quickly realized that even his prayers of thankfulness and intercession were being hindered because of his reluctance to talk to his wife. Remembering his commitment to move towards such "opportunities," he called Donna and arranged for a mid-afternoon coffee and snack at a nearby bistro. Donna was pleasantly surprised at the invitation and eagerly waited for her husband to get down to business after a few pleasantries.

"Honey, I want you to be completely honest with me about something. I know we have had a rough few days with the budget crisis and all. But as I was preparing for my Thanksgiving series I was struck with how much you and the kids mean to me, you know, how thankful I am for you and them. I really don't want us to keep on with this distance between all of us. What can I do to make this better? I really am trying to do the right thing, you know."

"Jerry, you are doing the right thing. But I have to tell you, honestly, that you are doing it in the wrong way. No, don't say anything yet, hear me out. It's one thing to stick to principles, even ones we've all agreed to. But principles don't trump people, especially your family, and especially their—I mean our—feelings. As an example, the vacation was a lot of fun for you and the kids, but I don't feel that you appreciated the sacrifice I was making by staying back from the activities so much. I felt I had to do it, given the situation. But that's just it, you created that situation and didn't realize the stress it was causing me. Just like you created the budget rules and couldn't see the stress it was causing the entire family.

"Sometimes principles and rules need to be adapted, or bent, or just plain broken. Especially when people are hurting. I know you are going to say that 'we' agreed to the budget rules, just like 'we' agreed to the camping and cooking-in 'vacation.' I went along, but you had to know it was not my heart's desire for a fun and relaxing time away. To be very honest, I still feel resentful of the time you had with the kids. I have tried not to let it bother me, but it did, and it does. That was the reason I changed my mind on wanting us to be with you at the cabin. I just wanted time to heal. And I prayed that you would see what was happening. You grew in a lot of ways those two weeks, but there was still a lot that didn't change. I guess this is a blind spot. Sometimes you have to ask others to show them to you. So there, you asked for honesty. Sorry?"

"No, I'm not sorry I asked, but yes, I am sorry for how I've hurt you. This is awful. I can't believe I missed the obvious. What happened? I mean, tell me how I let this happen? You and the kids are the most precious people in my life. I love them, and you especially, more than my own life. How did I get so out of whack?"

"I don't know. I think you need to take this to the Lord in prayer, and maybe get some additional help from someone you trust to see what is at the root of this and how to deal with it. I don't have to tell you that these are just recent examples. I've been stuffing such feelings most of our marriage, praying that things would get better. So if it's been hidden from you for so long, there must be reasons. Maybe the things you talked about with Mark can help. You know, hurts from the past. Developing a controlling attitude to protect yourself. Whatever. There's something at the bottom of this, and I know you can trust God to help you find out what it is and what to do about it."

Jerry committed to his wife that he would search out such an opportunity to discover the source of his frustration and subsequent inability to see the hurt he was causing Donna and the kids. He stopped working on his Thanksgiving message and spent the rest of the afternoon addressing the immediate need in his family. He worked out how they could draw on their long-term savings to cover the unexpected expenses, continue to support the seniors with missions gifts, and even get new shoes for everyone. They would use this situation to institute a larger emergency fund, and have a plan to build it up over the next year.

Then he spent time in prayer for each family member. He wanted to know how God felt about each of them, and to identify where he had hurt them with his stubbornness. And then, how to ask each one individually for forgiveness. He even decided to get them each a small gift as a sort of atonement for his sin. The more he thought about it, the more excited he became to give his fault in the matter back to the Lord and to humble himself before his family. He knew this was the right thing to do, and that God would greatly bless them all as a result.

The reconciliation with his family that night was miraculous. Jerry spoke heartfelt words admitting the hurt he had caused in the budget situation, the family "vacation," and other incidents. He apologized to each person and asked their forgiveness for hurting them and for his overall lack of sensitivity to their needs. He told them he had already found a weekend retreat ministry that would help him get to the root cause of the blindness that had contributed to his family's hurts.

But he took full responsibility, and promised to give them a detailed report on what he would discover at the weekend "encounter." The impact on the kids and Donna was immediate. They all recognized his sincerity and the humility it took to admit fault and apologize. It was not something they were used to hearing, and they quickly and enthusiastically forgave him with hugs and tears. They were especially grateful when he proposed the solution to the budget problem and committed to each one his desire to seek God's best for them.

# 13

## The Men's Group and Retreat

After reconciling with his family that night, and completing his Thanksgiving series preparation the following day, Jerry's next area of focus was the men's group and the first ever men's retreat. As he talked with George and prayed about the overall direction and how to start, he felt that he should first engage the small group of men that he and George had been mentoring. If it worked out, he would see them as leaders and coaches for the larger men's group, and they would help plan and execute the retreat. But first he needed to ramp up the mentoring group as a more organized entity. He called them together for a Saturday breakfast at the church. After the usual chatter and laughter, he got up to address them.

"Guys, thanks for coming out on your morning off. I know you have lots to do today, so I'll get to the point. We have had a good time in our Wednesday night class, and I believe we have gotten to know one another much better. I have enjoyed the teaching material, and based on our discussions, I know it has challenged you all to step up to the plate in your roles as men, whether as head of a family, or as one with influence at work and with your peers. It has helped me be more confident in my role as a husband, father, and example to other men. It's how God sees us and wants us to mature towards the destiny He has placed within our hearts.

"So I want to take the challenge a step further, beyond the teachings we have had and into practical application. If you are willing, I would like to continue with this group, but with a different, less structured purpose. That would be to engage one another in real life situations. By that,

I mean to find out what others are going through and praying for one another regularly and in depth. Also, that means following up and holding one another accountable for applying godly principles, such as the ones we have been learning. It's easy to learn and agree that we should be doing these things, but it's something else to apply them in the trials we face daily. It is hard to be real with others about our fears and struggles and victories.

"There's more, but before I go on, does anybody have any questions or thoughts?"

"Yes, Pastor Jerry," said Joe. Joe was a newcomer to the church, but who had jumped into the Wednesday night class and was fired up about his faith. "This is just what I've been hoping for. I'm not sure where you are going, but I really feel the need to get to know a few guys better and share life with them. I came from a very small church, as you know, so this group has already made me feel at home and cared for. But I still miss the intimate relationships with a few men where I knew a lot about them and we were very open about our challenges at work and with our relationships. I still call a couple of them regularly to get things off my chest and get their advice as I'm adjusting to my new location and job."

"Joe, I couldn't have asked for a better segue for what I have to say next. You have nailed it, my friend. So here's what I am proposing. I would like for us to keep meeting Wednesday nights as a group for continued teachings and sharing. But I challenge you to break into groups of three, four, or five and have weekly or semi-monthly sessions with a very simple agenda. The time spent would be no more than an hour and a half, and you would simply find out what has been happening in each other's lives, pray for one another, and commit to at least one action that you want to be held accountable for at the next session. The sharing time would include confession of any sin of omission or commission, and then praying for forgiveness. Someone would have the Lord's Prayer in front of them and encourage the group to touch on each point during the session, although that will probably become a natural thing to do. I plan to teach on how to do that on the next few Wednesday nights.

"Well, that's it in a nutshell. I don't want this to be too prescriptive, but I do want to encourage each group to let the Holy Spirit lead them in a way that will meet the needs of each person at each session. Questions, thoughts?"

Hands shot up as Jerry fielded questions, such as how to select the groups so no one would be left out, when and where to meet, whether to meet around a meal, who would lead, how to ensure confidentiality, and many more. Jerry continued to emphasize being flexible and not getting into a rut or legalism, but many found it helpful to hear ideas about how they could at least get started. Jerry suggested that if someone didn't want to participate at this time, that they could still come Wednesday nights, and then join a group whenever they were comfortable or their schedule would allow. He made it clear that this was strictly voluntary.

Over the next few Wednesday nights, Jerry gave examples of how to apply the sections of the Lord's Prayer to the meetings in a natural way. He even devoted a class to allowing one of the first groups to have an abbreviated meeting in front of the room. They shared ideas that could help other groups get started or go a bit deeper. Jerry also taught in one class about these accountability groups were modeled in church history and in other churches he was aware of. He emphasized the importance of these types of meetings and demonstrated that they can take many different forms tailored to meet the needs and times of each group. Over the centuries, such small groups devoted to prayer and accountability have been the foundation of major moves of God that produced lasting fruit.

A few weeks after the small groups had been meeting, Jerry asked at a Wednesday class for volunteers to help him and George James plan a winter men's retreat, and perhaps act as coaches for some exercises to lead the men into deeper relationships and accountability. Instantly, every man's hand shot up. Jerry was visibly moved, and the entire class recognized that God was doing something special in their hearts.

Jerry said, "Men, this is a turning point for our church. I knew this was the year to get serious with the men's ministry, and to have our first retreat. To be frank, I was dreading starting yet another program, especially one that had been attempted before without real success. I take the blame for that, but you have shown me that this is God's timing, not mine. He has done a work in your hearts, and it's time to share this experience with other men.

"So here's what I believe we should do. Let's devote the next two meetings to the retreat. The first will be to plan the general purpose, basic agenda, and type of facility. The second week will be to lay out the breakout sessions and the role you, as coaches, will play. George and I have some ideas we will present at each meeting, but I am totally open to changing it to be what this group believes will work best for our men. There is wisdom in many counsellors. So pray before each class and let's find God's will for making this a milestone event for our men and for our church. I will send you some thoughts we have shortly, and perhaps you can even discuss this at your small group meetings. I do ask you, though, to not hold too tightly to your ideas, as I plan not to. Let's give the Holy Spirit an opportunity to work during our next two classes. Let's watch Him bring out the best in us as we discuss ideas and then prayerfully decide on a course for this retreat. We can always use good ideas for future retreats as well. I am excited to see what will happen."

"Pastor Jerry," said Ricardo, "I appreciate your wanting to get the group's input on the retreat. But is it realistic to expect this many of us to come to a decision that everyone will like? I'm sure I speak for the others in saying that we trust you and George to lay this out, and we will support you."

"Ricardo, I hear what you are saying. I don't expect that everyone will like everything that comes out of this, and I realize that I have the final responsibility for what is decided. But I am ready to change the paradigm for how we do things around here, especially where we are breaking new ground. I want to—no, I need to—trust the Christ in you, each of you, all of you. How can we be members of the same body if we don't trust one another with important stuff? Does it really matter what the details of the retreat look like? Isn't the important thing to learn to love and trust each other with our souls, with our very lives? I think so.

"If there is one thing I learned on my sabbatical, it is that I have to first trust God with my fears, insecurities, and doubts. The way He tests my faith is to then see if I will trust Him enough to make myself vulnerable to others. The ultimate question is whether I can handle the thought of not being in control. If I can't, then how can I trust Him? It's not just about trusting you, it's about me trusting God and not being concerned about the results. The most important things that happened on my sabbatical would never have happened if I had set the agenda and not allowed others to speak into my life and challenge my cherished habits and beliefs. God is so much bigger than my theological or managerial principles. He refuses to fit within them, for my own good, and for the good of this church."

With one motion, every man in the class stood to his feet and began deliberately to applaud their pastor. At first with a slow tempo in unison, and then faster until they began shouting, "Yes, Lord, change us. Use us. We love You and worship You. You are mighty. Hallelujah."

Jerry smiled at the men, then looked heavenward and joined in their praise.

At the next class, Jerry presented a rough outline of a proposed retreat agenda. He started with an open discussion of the purpose of the retreat, reiterating his desire that this be about allowing men the opportunity to get closer to one another and to God. The main vehicle would be teaching, and then in small groups sharing their hurts and fears so they could pray for one another and build one another up. The ultimate purpose was to establish strong relationships that would last beyond the retreat. The agenda supported that with general teachings and small group exercises at a very personal level.

The class discussed the purpose and agreed, with one addition. They wanted to define lasting relationships in two ways. One would be to encourage the small groups to continue to meet regularly after the retreat, as those in the class had been doing. They also wanted to encourage one-on-one relationships, but were unsure how that could happen in a limited retreat setting. Jerry finally said that he agreed with the goal, but that such a personal level of relationships might best be left to the

Holy Spirit to manage. Perhaps the goal should be to provide teaching and opportunities for men to have some one-on-one time, say, based on interests or age levels, but that they wouldn't set any expectations. The exercises would be to illustrate the value of such relationships, but it would be up to the men to work things out on their own. They might choose to approach someone else, but at least they would understand the benefits and have some idea of what such relationships should look like. The key would be to go deeper than men normally do in understanding one another's wants and fears, and committing to praying for each other's spiritual and emotional growth.

The last item, the location and facility, was easy. George had found an ideal rustic resort facility that would provide dorm rooms and home cooking. The men were particularly excited when they reviewed the western-style menus and continuous snacks and drinks. A men's retreat is no time to start a diet. But to counter that, the grounds were spacious with lots of activity areas from cards, to basketball, to horseshoes and bank fishing. For a modest fee, there was even horseback riding and 4-wheeler trails. The whole class was enthusiastic and felt that the fees were reasonable. Several even offered to sponsor someone else who couldn't afford the full registration.

At the second class to plan the breakout sessions and coaches' role, Jerry started off with an agenda for the specific teaching topics and the discussion questions for the breakouts. As he was describing the teaching sessions, however, there was some stirring among the men. Finally, someone asked if in a retreat setting we shouldn't have shorter, less theological teachings and allow more time in the discussion groups. A couple of other men agreed and further suggested that the teaching time be primarily stories of personal experience, preferably light-hearted, even funny, although with a serious message.

Some in the room were a bit uncomfortable with what sounded like criticism of Jerry's teaching style, but Jerry took it in stride. He had determined beforehand that he was going to be very flexible and open to new ways of doing things. He chose immediately to embrace the suggestions and move enthusiastically toward them. He even asked George to take the session on building manly relationships, because everyone appreciated George's laid back style and hilarious stories of his early years. Characteristically, George tried to "aw shucks" his way out of it, but the men made such a fuss over him that he agreed to do it, with one condition. He asked Jerry to agree to an arm wrestling contest between the staff and the deacons to warm everyone up for his manly one-on-one stories.

Jerry again moved toward what might have been an awkward moment in earlier times, and challenged George to put his muscle where his mouth was right then and there. After a few raucous moments, the men cheered George. Just as he was about to pin Jerry's arm, he pretended that he pulled an arm muscle and fell out on the floor in mock agony. The men finally got back to their seats and quickly agreed on the breakout sessions. They asked if they could act out one session that was a bit unclear. Again, the players made the experience fun, but ended on a serious note that demonstrated the value of the teaching and group discussion. The entire class left buzzing about the retreat and spread the word quickly to their friends that they wouldn't want to miss this one, for the food if nothing else.

The men's retreat exceeded Jerry's wildest dreams. The men enjoyed the worship songs, the teaching time, testimonies, recreation, and of course the food. But almost everyone was touched deeply in his spirit through the breakout sessions where they practiced being vulnerable with one another, writing out incidents that had hurt them deeply, reading those aloud to their small groups, and then praying for forgiveness for those who had hurt them and for their own anger and bitterness. Other sessions dealt with identifying fears and anxieties and their root causes. They tried to recognize the sources, typically lies of the devil, and then renounce them.

Many of the men had heard teachings and sermons on these topics. While they thought they had addressed them in their thoughts or later in private prayer times, few had ever brought these out into the open. At the retreat, they were addressed through written and verbalized words, and then prayed earnestly, out loud. They agreed to hold themselves accountable to those same men on a regular basis. In the final session of the long weekend, almost every man stood before his group and told a heartfelt story of what God had done during the retreat. Many choked up, but most all were sincerely impacted, and clearly they were committed to a renewed inner and outward life.

The real testimony, however, was in the following weeks. Wives, family members, and friends saw a remarkable change in their husbands, fathers, and friends. They let Pastor Jerry and others know that they wanted to experience the same thing. A number of small groups that began with the retreat continued as men's study and accountability groups. Several of those, and others from the retreat, expanded to include spouses and friends.

There had been a few small groups already in place, coordinated by Mark Henson, mostly long time social gatherings of friends who had been in the church many years. The new groups took on the characteristics they had seen modeled at the retreat. Most of them decided to circle back on the teachings they had received and reviewed them so those who didn't attend the retreat had the same background. Depending on the day of the week and time, the groups decided on a rhythm of singing a couple of praise songs, having a short teaching with interactive discussion, praying for needs that had been submitted on prayer cards, and finally, enjoying snacks and fellowship. This sequence allowed those with children to leave after the prayer time, if desired.

Jerry devoted a sermon to the small groups, and encouraged anyone not involved in one to sign up and indicate their interests in an age-related group, a topical or interest group, a men's or women's group, or a group consisting of friends who already did things together. Jerry and Mark and their wives then arranged everyone who signed up into suggested groups, each with a volunteer leader and host home. They were to try the group for six months and then complete an anonymous evaluation of whether to continue with the same group or express an interest in joining another existing group. The understanding was that from then on, anyone could ask for a reassignment at any time, or could just continue in the group for as long as they wanted.

Occasionally at Jerry's staff meeting, the pastors and key staff would discuss how the small groups were working. Some were concerned that there was too much freedom to do whatever they wanted, and others were concerned that some of the group leaders were either too serious or not serious enough in including teachings and meaningful group discussion. As a result, Jerry asked Mark to meet annually with the leaders for a half-day workshop to instill a few basic objectives and share ideas on both what was working and on opportunities for improvement.

The biggest surprise was the growing request for people to attend the topical and interest groups. Jerry realized that these were popular because the church did not offer a full adult education program on Sundays or Wednesdays. After surveying the congregation about this and other topics, he decided to hire an adult education minister who would develop those programs, as well as help coordinate the small groups, which were becoming too numerous for Mark to give adequate supervision. As the small groups and adult education program matured, Jerry continued to emphasize them periodically in his sermons. He and Donna regularly visited a different one each month, as well as continuing to sponsor his men's mentoring group. As he sampled the variety of styles, he gained a fuller appreciation for how diverse and interrelated the body truly is. People found great satisfaction in having choices and being able to learn and serve in areas that fit their needs.

The final lesson Jerry and the staff learned was to get newcomers plugged into a group from the start. They took seriously the welcome card visitors filled out, and assigned a likely small group leader to follow up with each one within two days. The personal appeal to attend a small group was a big surprise to most visitors, and one they had trouble turning down when they realized that they would be in someone's home around people with similar interests. If the visitor hadn't completed all the interest questions on the welcome card, the leader asked about their interests during the call. They then passed the information to the appropriate leader.

The follow up process didn't stop there, though. If the visitor didn't return to church or didn't attend a small group within the next couple of weeks, the leader called them again to find out why and suggest a different small group. The discipline of following up continued when someone appeared to drop out for two or three weeks in a row. It continued until the person said they were attending elsewhere, shared they had moved out of the area, or asked not to be contacted. Even then, they were kept on the weekly mailing until they asked to be unsubscribed. Jerry was determined that no one would be neglected. Paying attention to visitors became a core value of the ministry. It contributed not only to a significant increase in the growth rate of the church, but modeled the care that each attender was expected to take with anyone who visited the church.

# 14

## The T-shirt Incident

About this time, a new family moved to the area and began attending the church. The Robertson's had bought a local fast food franchise, and soon became active in the community and in the church's ministries. They volunteered their house to host a new small group and attended the Wednesday couples class regularly. John Robertson was as gregarious as Betty was reserved. They complemented each other well in their restaurant, with Betty working the office and John training staff and building a loyal customer base. He offered to help the church when they needed low-cost catered meals, and as a result, saw many church members frequenting his restaurant.

One day, John asked Jerry to lunch to discuss a proposition. He wanted to sponsor the spring break missions trip that his two high schoolers were signed up for. He proposed to pay for the transportation for the entire team in return for them wearing nice t-shirts with his restaurant's name and logo on the back. Jerry wasn't sure about the idea, but decided to not react immediately. He thanked John politely and said he would consider it and visit with the staff about his proposal. After the meal, Jerry was disappointed with himself at not turning the offer down politely, but told himself that he needed to be careful not to offend his new members who had become well known in the church.

After mentioning the offer to Mark, he was a bit surprised that Mark seemed open to it. Mark said that John had asked him last week what he thought about helping the missions team, and that he had done something like this at his previous church. Mark didn't think much about it at the time, but suggested he talk to Pastor Jerry if he wanted to pursue it. Jerry told Mark that he thought it was not a good idea, and that the church didn't generally allow commercial advertising to support public ministry. Mark said he understood, but wondered what was different about the men's softball team who had sponsored t-shirts in return for covering field and umpire expenses. Jerry said that was different. Sports were just recreational and were not considered a ministry outreach like a missions trip. Mark said he could see that, but that it would sure help financially. Jerry responded that it just didn't feel right, and Mark backed off without really agreeing.

Jerry decided to talk to Donna about it that night. He didn't normally take routine things like this home, but he was concerned that maybe he was being legalistic and he needed her frank opinion. Donna agreed that it seemed to be a clear case of violating the advertising policy. But she suggested that before he got back with John, they should individually pray about it and then come back together to further pray and seek the Holy Spirit's guidance. She felt that there was something else going on that was causing this to have gone beyond a quick no thank you when John proposed it. Jerry reluctantly agreed, but he was afraid this was becoming a bigger deal than it should be.

When they came back together the next morning during their shared devotional time, Jerry asked Donna what she was hearing.

"Honey, I am not sure what is happening here, but I think this is more than a simple request. I think there is a manipulating spirit at work."

"OK. I trust your discernment, but I didn't really hear anything. What do you think I should do?"

"I don't know. I guess you need to discern that for yourself. I would be careful, though. I am not sensing that there is any intent to manipulate or deceive on John's part. I think you may need to spend more time asking for deeper wisdom here."

Jerry took his wife's suggestion seriously. He was curious that something so innocent and of small importance would be causing such concern on his part and minor confusion within his staff. Jerry decided to fast breakfast and lunch and spend the lunch hour in prayer about this one topic. As he began to ask for Holy Spirit wisdom and revelation, he quickly had the impression to call in his new volunteer prayer ministry leader. Janet was a retired pastor of a small rural church. She and her husband, Ron, had been attending for a year when he went on the men's retreat. Shortly after, she had approached Pastor Jerry about volunteering to help with prayer. He had just decided that the church needed to fill a part-time prayer minister position, so he took her offer as confirmation. It also was a blessing of God's provision that he was able to staff it with an experienced person at minimal cost.

Jerry quickly learned to appreciate Janet's seasoned wisdom and practical approach to the ministry. Her first step was to enlist a core of supporters who were already known as prayer warriors. Their job was to intercede for Janet, the prayer ministry, and the church. Her next step was to start a Tuesday night prayer service where she and Gabe worked together to create an atmosphere of prayerful worship for an hour, with Janet and others leading out every few minutes with short prayers on various topics. They always ended with prayer for the Wednesday and Sunday services.

Of more relevance to the current situation, though, was Janet's third step. She trained a larger group of prayer intercessors and prophetic prayer warriors. This last effort caused a minor stir in the congregation. Some thought it was a bit bold and unorthodox, and were concerned that these people would get out of hand and start prophesying, healing, and casting out demons every chance they got. However, Janet's training was biblically sound, and the class members were asked to practice first within the class, and then after finishing the class, as part of the altar ministry on Tuesday nights. This powerful personal prayer ministry, along with the anointed corporate prayer and worship, made Tuesday nights Jerry's favorite service, and he let the entire congregation know this in no uncertain terms.

When Jerry and Donna met with Janet and told her about John's t-shirt offer, she immediately was concerned. "Pastor, I am sensing exactly what Donna described. I agree it doesn't seem like a big deal, but there is definitely a wrong spirit behind this. John probably has no idea what is motivating him. Let me pray about this with one of my intercessors, if that's alright. I'll also ask the team to pray, without giving the details, that we will have clear discernment."

"OK, Janet, I trust you to pursue it and get back to me."

Then Donna interjected, "Why don't we pray right now, and agree on a quick resolution, but one that gets to the root of the discomfort we are feeling?" Janet agreed and led the three of them in a simple prayer, asking for the gift of discerning of spirits, and that truth would be revealed in an atmosphere of grace.

Two days later, Janet asked to meet with Jerry and Donna. She started by explaining that Helen, the other prayer warrior she told about the situation, without mentioning names, also had the same immediate reaction. Then, as they were praying together, both silently and aloud, Helen stopped for a few minutes and described a vivid impression she just had. It was the scene from 1 Kings 21 where Jezebel, the queen of Israel, convinced her husband, King Ahab, to confiscate their neighbor's vineyard and have him killed in the process. Helen knew then that the t-shirt incident was inspired by a Jezebel spirit of manipulation. It seemed a stretch to her, but the impression came immediately, and was so clear that she did not doubt the meaning. Janet said that they then prayed against this spirit, and after a while, began to sense that something had shifted. Helen believed that the spirit was trying to get a foothold in the church, and that this was just a first baby step to insinuate itself. She and Janet both felt that it had been resisted, and that it had left, probably to try again in some other way, or perhaps to go down the street and try a different church. Janet smiled at the last part, and said, "Just kidding."

Jerry and Donna thanked her, and Jerry led a simple prayer of agreement that the spirit of Jezebel was cast out, and also that it not return. He said, however, that this just shows the value of a prayer ministry, and especially of a praying wife who is not hesitant to raise an issue about something so insignificant that she felt was wrong. He said that this is exactly the kind of diligence and sensitivity that would be needed by all of the prayer team to fend off the devil's schemes to distract and discredit the church. He was committed to supporting this ministry and taking seriously any warnings they raised.

A week later, John came to Jerry and apologized that he would not be able to follow through on the offer to pay for the mission team's transportation. His wife had finished the books for the month, and they were experiencing an unusual slump that would require him to hold off on any discretionary spending. Jerry offered his condolences on the business problems, and assured John that he would be praying for a quick recovery and that he would be happy to accept whatever offering they could eventually manage. He also told John that it was probably just as well, since the church board had recently passed a resolution about limiting advertising sponsors to recreational sport events, and that missions trips and other ministry events would only be supported by designated offerings. John seemed a bit puzzled, but quickly excused himself, and said he would definitely consider that in the future. Jerry immediately told Donna and Helen about this clear answer to their praying against the Jezebel spirit.

# 15

## The Organic Church Revealed

The T-shirt incident, as Jerry referred to it in his own mind, became a milestone of sorts. He resolved to do two things as a result. One was to not take seemingly insignificant feelings or questions for granted, but to put every situation before the Lord and ask for wisdom about what to take seriously and what to leave alone. He was reminded that King David regularly asked questions about which path to take before going into battle. His motto became, "Just Ask, and then Just Do It."

The second was to depend more on other people, especially trusted advisers such as his wife, pastors, and board members. He had seen the value of being open to what others had to contribute during his sabbatical. He was pleasantly surprised at how God used his visitors to bring thoughts that were uncharacteristic for them, and challenging to him. It was as if the Holy Spirit was saying to give his associates more freedom, and to watch God move through them for even greater good than he could have imagined.

Jerry was at first uncomfortable with releasing people in this way. His old controlling nature, as well as his training and counsel from pastors' conferences, had always emphasized the need to maintain order and a healthy respect for the lead pastor's authority in a local body. But he had seen that role time and again be unintentionally, and sometimes intentionally, abused. He even noticed signs of abuse in himself. Some were obvious, such as being offended and jealous when a prominent member or staff person announced they were "being led" to go elsewhere. He knew it was natural to be hurt, but it took very little to let that go into a personal offense. He was very good about having a generous outward attitude, such as sending them off with the church's blessing, and even with a gift of appreciation for their service. But deep down he was hurt that they hadn't come to him first. With the few who had talked to him first, his impulse was to talk them out of it. He knew that this was hypocritical, but it seemed so defensible.

Then there were other less obvious temptations, such as overworking staff in the name of ministry excellence. Again, deep down he knew that he was really manipulating them by appealing to their natural desire to please. But although the short term results seemed to justify this subtle form of abuse—for the good of the ministry—the longer term impact on individual and family stress levels was noticeable. Again, Jerry could almost justify this behavior because he put the same stress on himself, but he had to admit that he was experiencing symptoms of fatigue, irritability, and strained relationships, especially even recently with his family.

Jerry decided that these issues were of such importance that he took several days off to return to the lake cabin to seek God's guidance about his relationships with staff, church members, and his family. He studied 1 Corinthians 12, Romans 12, and Ephesians 4, among others. He had taught on these passages many times to emphasize that each person needed to find their place in the body and that we need to support one another in being the best at what God has called us to be. As he meditated on these familiar verses, however, he felt there was more, much more.

He saw, for example, that all men everywhere can see clearly the evidence of a Creator, but it is only by faith that people come to believe in a personal God who works in the details of their lives to redeem, restore, and call them to a divine, eternal purpose. Likewise, it is only by faith that members of Christ's body can receive the gifts and ministry functions designed for them by God and distributed through the Holy Spirit. And it is further by faith that the members of the body of Christ can operate in those gifts for the best overall good of the body, because that is how the body is designed. Therefore, since this is all discerned and understood by faith, there is no point in trying to analyze why one member has certain gifts and another has different gifts and functions. This is the first level of accepting the way God made us and not comparing ourselves to others, which can lead to jealousy and strife.

The next level of understanding the makeup of the body is to realize that, even if we have the same gifts and function as someone else, they will be used in very different ways based on their specific calling for His purpose. This is where comparison becomes more tempting. We recognize that a friend has similar gifts, such as words of understanding and knowledge, and they fulfill a similar purpose in the church, such as a teacher. It might then be tempting to ask why one is asked to teach the large couples Sunday school class, while the other is asked to teach a small class on prayer. Is one being given preference over the other? Or are both fulfilling needed roles in the church at a point in time and in a way that makes best use of their talents? But then the question arises, who gets to decide who should teach what class? And do they have to explain their decisions? How many sincere people with a teaching gift, or a musical talent, or other skills have left a church because they weren't being given the opportunities they felt they deserved?

Jerry grimaced as he pondered this issue, having faced it multiple times in many areas of the ministry, both with staff and with volunteers. He had always been puzzled by the hurt people felt when they thought they weren't able to exercise their gifts in the way they thought they should. And then there were others who didn't think they had any gifts and felt they were doing their duty by just showing up and giving in the offering.

But the distribution and exercise of gifts was just one issue that caused problems between members of the body. There were others, such as physical appearance, personality characteristics, earning ability, mental sharpness, energy level, and even sense of humor. The list was almost as varied as individuals. Why is there so much diversity and variation in the body of Christ, much less in the human race? How can we ever have unity with so much potential for differentiation, and therefore division?

The most puzzling example of all is the paradox that opposites attract. Why is that? Why do couples so often have such different characteristics? One is an introvert and the other an extrovert. One is task oriented and mechanically minded and is critical of the other for not seeing how things should be done. One is relational and sensitive to people and is critical of the other for being stern and demanding, especially towards children. One likes to be on time and the other couldn't be bothered. One plans ahead and the other lives in the moment. And all of these differences are a constant source of stress. One of Jerry's best pastor friends and his wife go to church in separate cars. It isn't, as you might think, because the pastor needs to be at church early. Instead, it is because his wife does. He takes calls and tweaks his sermon notes right up until the service is about to start. But they have recognized their differences in ministry strengths, and after some early years of arguing, have developed a simple schedule accommodation that works for them.

So, if God designed us to be so different, how does He expect us to live and work together in unity, and love, even? It's easy to say we just need to appreciate one another's uniqueness, but when it comes down to it, those differences lead to competition, envy, pride, insecurity, guilt, and all sorts of stress. What is the solution?

As Jerry's thoughts reached this climax of concern, he almost became anxious. He knew intellectually that diversity was part of God's plan, and he enjoyed the variety of creation and people himself, but he hadn't really thought about the negative aspects as much. After all, we live, work, and play in this environment, and, sure, it causes some problems, but we try to make the most of it. So, he automatically asked in prayer, "What is the solution?"

As soon as he asked, he began to get a download of Holy Spirit wisdom. He saw that Romans 8:28 was the key. "And we know that all things work together for good to those who love God, to those who are the called according to His purpose."

The emphasis in this verse is typically on the phrase "all things work together for good," and it is used to let believers (those who love God) know that God is in control and will use even the seemingly most difficult circumstances to further His ultimate redemptive plan for their lives. But Jerry's attention was drawn to the end of the verse, "called according to His purpose." This is typically taken to mean that the verse applies to those who are called out, elected, according to God's plan, or in other words, those who are saved.

But earlier the verse identifies that this is for "those who love God," so the final qualifying phrase must mean more. In fact, it refers as well to the purpose for which God has called the believer, their "purpose in life" or their "destiny." This is getting personal. So many Christians continue to ask and wonder what their purpose is. They are rightly not satisfied with a generality, such as to love God and to love others, and then do whatever their circumstances dictate, or what someone asks them to do. Certainly, loving and serving God and others is what they are commanded to do in all their thoughts and relationships, but what are they supposed to be "doing" with their life? Isn't there something more specific that God has called them to—their "purpose?"

Jerry had brought in a program that Mark taught for new members to understand their personality characteristics and motivational gifts; however, few people who went through it took the last step to write down their specific, personal purpose in life. Jerry had wondered about this, but got vague answers from people such as, "Well, it's easy for ministers to know what your purpose is, it's your life work, and it ties directly to the commands of the Bible to preach the word and to make disciples. But is my purpose my job? Is my destiny to be a salesman? A programmer? A mother? Really?"

Jerry decided right then to work with the staff to develop a follow-up class that would focus on revealing a believer's specific purpose. He felt the Holy Spirit saying that it was a major source of frustration and confusion in the body. Teachers typically focused on the ministry gifts mentioned in Romans 12 and 1 Corinthians 12, but lay people assumed these were just for church services, small group mini-services, and personal and family devotions. They didn't seem to apply to their working lives or their interactions with people outside the Christian community.

Jerry saw that there is a way to determine a person's God-given purpose and then integrate it with all aspects of their life. It's basically just a matter of asking for a rhema word from the Holy Spirit. But first the believer must be prepared to ask in faith and then understand what to do with the answer.

Preparing to ask such a powerful question is important. The believer needs to understand what they are asking for, that it is legitimate, and that God wants them to have the answer now. It's kind of like asking to be saved or to be filled with the Holy Spirit. It sounds daunting, but once you realize it's God's will for you and that you don't have to wait on any preconditions, you just do it by faith. So the first step is to teach people that it is God's will for them personally and to show this from the Bible, as in Hebrews 11:6, Jeremiah 1:5, and Galatians 1:15.

They should then be ready to act on the answer. Just as we counsel people what to do after salvation or being filled with the Spirit, we need to help them understand how to apply the words that they hear from the Holy Spirit. Of course, the Holy Spirit will give them continuing guidance, but they can benefit from teaching that helps overcome fear or doubt about knowing and acting on such an important revelation.

But knowing your purpose is just one step. The fuller meaning of Romans 8:28 is recognizing and cooperating with God as He orchestrates "all things to work together for good." This is where the deeper meaning of "all things" comes in, and where it relates to members of the body. "All things" is not just circumstances, but it includes people who are in your sphere of activity. And it is not just their impact on you. It means that you are part of a system, or body, where you not only have a specific purpose, or function, but that function is designed to work in perfect cooperation with other people, each of whom have their complementary functions.

As a believer, you can be assured that God has surrounded you with the perfect people and circumstances to allow you to fulfill the purpose He has for you. You just need to see it by faith and walk towards it, one step at a time. It helps to walk in an attitude of rest and waiting on God's timing, as Jerry had learned during his sabbatical talk with Bob Newcomb.

That doesn't mean that everything or everyone is going to help you in every way they can. Wouldn't that be nice? But it does mean that you will have divine opportunities to exercise your gifts and talents, along with your faith, to fulfill your purpose.

What does this have to do with members of the body? It means that each one has been uniquely designed to fulfill their God-given purpose, but only in concert with the others who make up their spheres of activity. Of course, there are many such concentric and overlapping spheres. First, you, then your close family, then your extended family, then your small group and church, then your workplace, then your community, region, nation, and finally the world and the body of Christ that is involved in each of these larger spheres. Within each of these spheres, we have a responsibility to seek out our specific role and how we can work with others to further our purpose, knowing that at the same time we will be helping others fulfill theirs.

Jerry decided that if this concept was from God, he should be able to find out what his role was. He knew that he had been called to fulltime ministry, especially to preach and teach. But he realized that he had never asked for anything more specific as a life purpose. He had always assumed he was to find a place in a church and use his gifts as he had opportunities. He had started, as many do, as a volunteer youth leader, and then became the youth pastor of a small church.

Because of his success in that role, a larger church called him to lead their youth and college age groups. This was a challenge, but Jerry knew how to build teams and delegate, so he was very successful. By the time he was only 30, he got a call from his current church, which at the time was a small, but fast-growing, church whose founding pastor had been forced to leave after a moral failure. Jerry was able to pull together the factions that had developed and avoid the church split that everyone had forecast. In fact, the church never went down in membership or offerings. Jerry had worked very hard to make this happen, and the recent building program and sabbatical were the board's and congregation's way of saying thank you for a job well done.

Jerry knew that he had received unusual revelations that were not just for him, but for the people in his church. They had a role they were to play in the community, and he felt that the lessons of wholeness and humility he had been learning were preparing them all for something important. So he positioned himself that night to ask in faith about his purpose. He texted Donna and asked her to contact Janet and a few key people to pray for special courage and wisdom. He had a light meal and turned on his favorite praise and worship music. After a while, he lowered the volume and began giving thanks for God's provision and care. He then, as was his custom, asked God to search his heart and show him anything he needed to repent of.

He was taken aback with the result. First, he felt an unusual and overwhelming presence of the Holy Spirit, filling him with a sense of the Father's love and friendship. His heart was overflowing with love for others, and he interceded for several friends, staff, and family. He then sensed that the Holy Spirit wanted to do a deeper work of repentance than normal. He began to see specific areas of sin. He was reminded of recent incidents that revealed pride, mistrust, fear, jealousy, impatience, anger, and on and on. These were not just ministry related incidents, but within his family, especially his wife. It also related to his interactions with the community, and even what he was putting on social media. He supernaturally understood the severity of the consequences of his words, actions, and inaction. He saw the Father's heart weeping for the harm that had been done, and his own heart began to break. He flung himself on the bare floor and sobbed uncontrollably. He finally cried out, "It's too much! What do I have to do to fix this?"

He heard the answer loud and clear, although softly and tenderly, "Jerry, I already fixed it on the cross. You know that, but I wanted you to have a fresh revelation of the effect of sin, even the slightest sins of omission."

"Why, Lord? It is so painful, and I know there is nothing within me that can make things right or even stop me from repeating my behavior. I am, as Paul said, the chief of sinners. I have been given so much, and look how I have blown it."

Finally, the Holy Spirit whispered, "Jerry, didn't you have something you wanted to ask?"

Now Jerry was having whiplash. One minute he is despairing of ever being useful in the kingdom, and the next he is being prompted to ask about his life purpose. "Why, Lord? Why is this the time to ask? I am so unworthy!"

"Yes, you are, Jerry. But you have called on My grace and mercy. You have asked forgiveness based on what Christ did for you on the cross. You have held nothing back. Now I will hold nothing back from you. What would you like Me to do for you?"

"Lord, you know before I even ask, but I say it for my sake. What is my specific life's purpose? What have You created and fashioned me to be and to do?"

Jerry wasn't expecting the full minute of silence that followed. Finally, he heard the words, "Feed My sheep."

"Yes, Lord, as You said to Peter. I also am a pastor of sheep and have been doing my best to feed them. What specifically do I need to be doing, or doing differently?"

"Jerry," the Lord said, "I want you to feed My sheep organically."

"Seriously?" chuckled Jerry. He was used to the divine sense of humor, but this was a serious matter. "OK, there must be something really deep in that. What do You mean, organically?"

"Jerry, your purpose is to shepherd this flock so they are prepared for the last days. And those days are coming even sooner than you think."

This got Jerry's attention. "OK, how do I do that? I've preached several messages on the End Times and the Second Coming already."

"Yes, and I want you to feed your sheep daily so they can take the teachings and apply them in every aspect of their lives. Your flock is not just a collection of individual people. They are called together, to this church, for a purpose, for such a time as this."

"Uh, that's pretty heavy, Lord. I'll bet most of them don't remember ten percent of what I've already taught. There may not be much to work with."

"That's why you have to feed them organically."

"What does that mean? No pesticides, harsh chemicals, genetically modified food, right? I can see spiritual analogies with those. Is that what You mean?"

"Yes, and more. But feeding them is not just about the food they take in. It's even more about how they assimilate and process that food and how they promote the building of their own bodies through exercise and other disciplines."

"Ah, now I get it. Disciplines. I have also taught endlessly on the disciplines of Christian growth and living."

"But is it working? Are you seeing the results in your people and how they interact with one another and the world?"

"OK, I'll stop justifying myself, and listen."

The Lord seemed to chuckle, and continued, "Well, Jerry, let's work on the word 'organic'. You know how much I like to take words apart and put them back together."

"Yes, You do. And so do I. I'm all ears."

"Well, your flock is like—no—it is, an organism. It is a living, breathing thing that has a purpose, just as the individual members, yourself included, each has a purpose."

The Lord continued to dialog with Jerry about His design of the organic church. He started with the picture Paul painted in 1 Corinthians 12. The body is made up of many organs and parts, each with a purpose, but none sustainable on its own. They are all designed to work together for a larger, higher, purpose. It is the same, as Paul pointed out, with the church. It is tempting to think that each member is self-sufficient. They certainly appear to be made that way. But even Adam needed a helper. He had a job to do, and he needed encouragement and support. But he needed something more. He needed to be able to relate to God in a very personal way. What better way than to share his life with a partner who also was filled with God-breathed life and purpose? Together, they could explore, not just the wonders of creation, but the mysteries of life. They could talk to one another about their dreams and goals, calling on God to help them understand how to live to the fullest, and then work together to see their aspirations fulfilled.

They were more together than they could ever be apart. Their kind, in fact, depended on their coming together for the purpose of bearing and raising children, who would then continue the process of living to support one another. This was the perfect picture of a healthy organism, where all parts work in harmony, not just for the greater good. That implies that somehow each individual is sacrificing something so that the others who are deficient can have their due. No, an organism cannot live, much less thrive, without interdependence among the members. The members will not just be diminished if they cannot function with this mutuality. They will die.

Of course, when sin entered the picture, there arose the opportunity for relationships to be broken, with one another and with God. How did Satan do this? By separating Adam and Eve from God and from one another. By sowing doubt and unholy desires, he lured them into a strained relationship in which distrust, envy, and pride could grow and spread. It was a familiar pattern for Satan. It was the same thing he had done to God. And God knew that he would do the same thing to any other creation.

But God had a plan. He designed His new creation to be better than the angels. He designed it to be weak and vulnerable. To Satan, but also to one another, and to God. And it was this vulnerability, this dependence on one another, that would provide the unity of purpose and strength to overcome the devil's schemes.

Jerry appreciated these principles, but was eager to see how they played into his purpose and the purpose of each of his church members.

The Holy Spirit continued to give Jerry understanding. He saw that interdependence was not a constraint to work within, but a life-giving force that brought energy and strength to the body. But how does this work with each member having their own purpose? Won't that be a source of strife and competition for attention and resources? The Holy Spirit assured Jerry that all things work together, but Jerry wanted to know how this works and what part each person plays. Are we supposed to just rock along and be driven by circumstances?

Of course not. Just as in the ideal market economy, as long as there is trust and a free flow of communication, Adam Smith's "Invisible Hand" will provide all the signals and information needed to maximize everyone's potential. Of course, this also assumes that people are primarily moral and rational, which is not always a good assumption. This is a non-coincidental metaphor for how the Holy Spirit works in our lives, and the same keys apply—having a purpose, then working that out in an atmosphere of trust and authentic communication. And hopefully the body of Christ operates in a highly moral and mostly rational manner!

It seems too simple, thought Jerry. Yes, it's so simple that people miss it. The devil is quite good at his job, so all he has to do is taint the flow of trust and communication. He also can attack the foundations of our moral behavior and rational mind. Of course, his main weapons are lies. He just has to get us to believe a lie, however small, that will cause us to question whether we can trust someone else to behave in a way that we expect. Doubt and fear are the key tools he uses. Then, as must happen with weak and vulnerable creatures, we are disappointed. We lose trust, which causes the body to be diminished, and it hurts us in the process. Mistrust then affects our communications with one another, with ourselves, and with God. Our fears and doubts encourage us to jump to conclusions about what someone else is saying. We discount even God's Word as we filter it through our disappointments in others, in ourselves, or in God's promises that don't seem to be fulfilled.

Jerry took a deep, unexpected breath at this last thought. He was filled with shame at his own feelings of disappointment in what looked like many unfulfilled promises he had been given over the years. Where were the mighty moves of God, the healings, and the shifts in the culture that had been prophesied, for his church, and the church at large? He had to admit in that second that he, too, harbored doubts about the truth of

God's logos and rhema words because of such disappointments. Jerry held his breath for another second, and then let it out, along with another round of uncontrollable tears that quickly became a flood of regret and repentance.

"God, I am so sorry for doubting Your Word and the words of Your godly people. Forgive me. Show me the depths of my sin and cleanse me of the stain of the enemy's lies."

As Jerry continued to weep and cry out, the Holy Spirit flooded his mind with the washing of the Word. Scripture after scripture came into his spirit and began slowly healing his wounds of rejection and inadequacy. He realized that he had allowed doubts to form, not because of a lack of faith in God, but because of a lack of faith in God's love for him. He was painfully aware of his weaknesses and fears, and deep down did not really believe that God could use him until he was a better preacher, a better father and husband, a better man. How could God use someone who had at his core feelings of unworthiness and insecurity?

"Jerry."

"Yes, Lord."

"I love you, son."

"I know, Lord."

"Do you really know how much I love you?"

"No, I'm sure I don't."

The Holy Spirit downloaded words and feelings of love that overwhelmed Jerry once again. As the tears subsided, he began to glimpse the depth of God's love that extended to him personally, and that Jesus had already paid the inestimable price, not just for his salvation, but also for his perfection in wholeness. There was nothing else that needed to be done. Jerry just needed to trust in what God had already done and rest in that assurance. Jerry smiled at the impossibility of the thought. Really? Nothing else I need to do? Just rest? He knew it was truth, but it still seemed so idealistic, so unrealistic.

"Lord, help my unbelief!"

# 16

## The Organic Church Made Real

Jerry returned from the lake cabin with renewed purpose and quiet vigor. He knew there would be no simple solutions. He knew that after this mountaintop experience he would quickly descend into the valley of real life. But he also knew that he had laid hold of eternal truths. He knew that he would pray, think, and act on the unfolding revelation of stewarding his sheep organically. The prospect actually excited him. He had never thought of his role in that way, and the specificity of his holy charge at once amazed and energized him. He enjoyed a challenge, and this would stretch and exercise all aspects of his being. Over the next few months, he realized the extent and depth of the change in perspective this simple concept made even in his routine activities.

Jerry's first action was to design opportunities for his staff to recognize how their areas interacted with, and depended on, the other parts of the ministry. He resisted the urge to research and teach on what he had heard about relating organically to one another, and instead he decided to rely on the Holy Spirit to teach through experience and group interaction—organically. He called a half-day workshop of the age-related ministries—children, youth, college and young adult. He challenged them to work out how they could best develop their members to mature and be ready for the next age level. He gave them very little direction, but prayed with them for wisdom and unity of purpose. He then surprised them all by leaving and saying that he wanted a ten minute presentation from each age group minister at the end of the day, and then he would lead a discussion to solidify their results. He said that whatever the group decided would be their direction for the new Christian Education term beginning in a few months.

The ministers and their key leaders were unsure how to begin after he left, but they soon warmed to the idea of having not only the responsibility, but the freedom to work together. After another heartfelt and humble prayer for wisdom, they jumped into a rapid fire discussion of vision, objectives, and methodologies. They were pleasantly surprised at how well their ideas flowed and complemented one another. They realized that each age group could identify goals for preparing their students for the next level only if they knew what that next age group's objectives were. They also decided that, since many of their students' siblings were in different age groups, they would benefit from occasionally having common themes that would encourage interaction in the homes.

Of course, this was all going to require coordination and work throughout the year, but they saw that having a general plan would actually make their weekly lesson and service planning easier. Then one of the leaders suggested that they ask Pastor Jerry if they could even coordinate some lessons and activities with his sermon themes, at least in general terms. They particularly thought that illustrations and object lessons could be coordinated in this way, with each age group explaining the principles appropriately for their audience.

To test the concept, they took the recently announced sermon series on forgiveness, and decided to use the story of Joseph as the common thread. The pre-school leader thought they could act out the part about Joseph being his father's favorite and illustrate how the other brothers and sisters must have felt. The elementary leader suggested they talk about Joseph's dreams, which would also bring out the attitudes of the other family members, and maybe look at how Joseph could have handled their responses with a little more humility. The youth leaders felt their age group could handle the scene where some of the brothers wanted to kill Joseph, but the more responsible ones tried to at least keep him from physical harm. They thought the emotions and thought processes would be complex enough to challenge even the upperclassmen to express their feelings as they identified first with the brothers and then with Joseph. Finally, the college and young adult leaders saw that the incidents around Potiphar's wife and the prison scenes would be good examples of handling difficult life situations with godly responses. After they congratulated themselves on working together so well and learning from one another, they took a break and then broke into the age groups to prepare their presentations.

Jerry was flabbergasted at the quality and depth of the presentations and congratulated the group on a job well done. Then he revealed the real purpose of the workshop. He led them in a discussion of how this exercise had helped them realize their dependence on one another and how they thought this could help them in their ministries in the next few weeks and months. By this time, the leaders were fired up and could hardly stop talking about the creative ideas that had flowed out of their group exercise. Some admitted they were skeptical that the pre-school leaders would have much to learn or contribute from the college and young adults, but the opposite happened. The young adult leaders had preschoolers themselves and were eager to give ideas and see how their college and young adults could benefit from the simple truths that were being suggested for the youngest children.

As the discussion wound down, Jerry thanked everyone for their energetic input and admitted that he also was a bit skeptical about the value in having such a wide range of interests working together. But he was also pleasantly surprised at the results and committed to having more interactive group exercises in the future, perhaps with other functions in the church, such as facilities maintenance, the business office, and the Sunday morning worship ministries.

Everyone agreed that they saw benefits, and they were especially eager to visit with the facilities maintenance teams since they affected everything that happened in the church and set the atmosphere of cleanliness and order. The pre-school leader joked that she wanted to personally shake the hands of the ladies who cleaned and sanitized the toys and cribs before and after each service. They deserved a lot of respect. Jerry took note and realized that these kinds of sessions were not just about generating good ideas, but even more importantly, about encouraging one another. Most workers got very little affirmation, especially the paid ones who served behind the scenes with little visibility or credit. It would be gratifying for them to see how much they are valued by the others.

Jerry would never have thought of having these types of people together in the same meetings. It would have sounded like a sure recipe for a gripe session. But he had learned first-hand that people appreciate having an opportunity to interact with one another about how best to minister. He also learned that it is not necessary to make such interactions too structured or to worry about what might be said without tight controls.

He was learning that this supernatural organism, called the church, was pretty creative, capable, and resilient if given the chance. He realized that he had discouraged such interactions in the past, not just because of the time involved, but because of the uncertainty in what might happen and the lack of control of the process. He now saw that the Holy Spirit was well able to orchestrate a beautiful harmony if trusted with the opportunity.

After the kids had gone to bed that evening, Jerry told Donna about what had happened. She was surprised at the risk he took by having the meeting, and even more so by the results. She immediately began to think of ways to get her women's ministry and the young marrieds' class to have similar interactions with other groups. One idea was to have the nursery and pre-school teachers do a panel discussion for the young marrieds about getting their children in the right mood for the class time, and then how to follow up after the class. Of course, there would also be a lot of questions from the young couples about other child raising situations, which would be the real benefit of the class. Plus, the couples would see the workers as more than just babysitters, but as co-laborers in raising their children. It would help form friendships based on mutual respect and interest in their children.

For the women's ministry, Donna asked Jerry if he thought there would be a possibility of having a similar panel discussion with some of the men's ministry leaders. He said, "Of course, but what would be the topic?"

She joked about having them tell one thing they wished most that their wife would do for them. Jerry smiled at that, but then said, "You know, I think that's a great idea. It will create some humorous opportunities, but I think everyone will be surprised at what comes out."

Donna asked him, "Well, what is one thing you wish that I would do for you?" He thought for just a few seconds, and then said carefully, "Just that you would always think the best of me and assume that I am doing what I think is best for you and the children."

Donna was taken aback, but quickly understood what Jerry was saying. Like most men, Jerry's biggest need was to be respected and trusted. Like most women, Donna was naturally skeptical of the male capacity for engaging at the emotional level she felt she needed. She admitted to herself that she often expected Jerry to notice things more, especially her subtle clues about how she was feeling and what she was thinking. When he didn't fulfill her expectations, she thought that he must have other motives or perhaps just did not care. She realized that she was creating an atmosphere of distrust that resulted in a self-fulfilling prophecy.

What if she did assume that he was doing the best he could to take care of her needs and those of the children? Maybe that trust would allow him to feel more freedom in sharing with her and being more sensitive to her needs rather than feeling mistrusted and defensive. OK, she would give it a try.

As he drifted off to sleep that night, Jerry reflected on how simply giving people an opportunity to share their thoughts and feelings was a powerful way to build trust and communication, the keys to a healthy organism. He wondered what other secrets of organic growth he would uncover in the days ahead.

# 17

## The End Times Teacher

Jerry didn't have long to wait to learn another lesson. And it was not at all what he was expecting. A week later Mark Henson barged into Jerry's office unannounced. "Pastor, we have a problem with the adult education program! I can't believe it."

"Slow down, Mark. What happened?"

"Well, you know John Smith, the End Times teacher who has been so popular with his Wednesday night class? Well, he has gone and done it now. He really went off the deep end, and I have a mutiny on my hands. You gotta help me with this one."

"OK, Mark, tell me about it. Start at the beginning."

"Sure. Well, he has been going through the book of Daniel, you know, and he was teaching about the meaning of Nebuchadnezzar's dream in Chapter 2, you know, the one about the image of a man made of gold, silver, bronze, and iron and clay, which represent the kingdoms of Babylonia, Medo-Persia, Greece, and Rome."

"Sure, pretty standard stuff. Did someone have another idea?"

"Wait. You haven't heard this part. He then mentioned in passing verse 43 about the iron mixed with ceramic clay, the part about 'they will mingle with the seed of men: but they will not adhere to one another.' He said that one interpretation was that the iron could be a return of the Nephilim of the Old Testament, supposedly the result of fallen angels or demons producing hybrid children through human women. Then he went on a tangent about how these Nephilim could be the source of deception that other New Testament verses warn about, and maybe even the Antichrist could be such a creature. Kind of a Rosemary's Baby scenario.

"I mean, that is controversial enough in the context of Old Testament teachings. But to bring that into today's times with an obscure reference in Daniel, well, it just set several of the class members off. They stormed into my office first thing this morning and respectfully demanded that I talk to John about being more careful in his teachings, and that he apologize to the class for getting off into non-biblical territory."

"So what is your plan, Mark?"

"My plan? I'm not the theologian here, that's your job, Pastor! My plan is to let you handle this one. And besides, one of the people who complained is on your board and another is the wife of a board member. So this is going to get around in an influential group. In fact, I bet it already has."

"Hmm. I see your dilemma. OK, I'll take this one off your hands. Give me any more details you have, and I will first take this to the Lord in prayer. I may try to get the group who came to see you back together later today or tomorrow before this goes much further."

After Mark and Jerry finished the debriefing, Jerry closed his office door and did some quick research on the topics Mark had mentioned. He found that, while there were a few similar teachings on the Internet, this was certainly not a mainstream or even a popular alternative interpretation. Then, as he had promised Mark, he prayed about this situation, asking for wisdom to understand the correct interpretation and also how to approach the people involved and to bring about a resolution. He was not at all prepared for what he heard.

"Jerry."

"Yes, Lord, I am listening."

"I want you to do a little more research."

"OK, Lord. About what?"

"Not what, but whom. I want you to thoroughly research what the different views today are regarding the antichrist."

"OK. May I ask why?"

"It's just an exercise. I want you to see something, but it will be best for you to experience it from a broad perspective."

"OK. Should I do this now? I'm behind in my final preparation for Sunday's sermon, and need to get the notes to the A/V team later today. But, of course You know that."

"Yes, now, Jerry. This will actually have a bearing on your sermon. I wouldn't ask you to do something without a reason."

"Oops, sorry for asking. Of course not. I'll get right on it."

"Jerry, this is going to be a very valuable lesson. Take it seriously. It will be resolved more quickly than you expect."

After an hour of reviewing commentaries and Internet references, Jerry prayed, "OK. Lord, I've done the research, at least I think it's enough given this situation. What's next?"

"So what did you find out, Jerry?"

"Well, the ideas about the Antichrist are all over the map. I wouldn't even say there is a mainstream position currently. The Pope was the mainstream candidate for centuries, but that doesn't seem to be so these days. There are so many other possibilities."

"Jerry, did you find much about the Antichrist being one of the Nephilim, or being related to them?"

"Not really. One or two speculations, but no one seems to have thought much along those lines. In fact, the phrase in Daniel about "mingling with the seed of men" was minimized or completely overlooked by most commentators. That was surprising. I also read a little more about the Nephilim and again found few commentators who gave them much attention in relation to end times. I think they are seen as strictly Old Testament figures, and a bit shadowy even at that."

"So what do you think the next step is, Jerry?"

"Well, I was hoping You could shed some light on this dilemma, Lord. I've done what I can do, so I would like for You to give me wisdom about how to resolve this."

"OK. I prefer not to get into the Nephilim issue any more. That is a mystery that it is not yet time to reveal. However, I will give you wisdom to resolve the situation. Just call the group together this afternoon. They will make it a priority. Oh, and by the way, call in John Smith at the same time."

"Uh, are You sure, Lord? OK, sorry for asking. Silly question. Yes Sir."

Jerry did not feel that he should ask for any more details about how to prepare or what to say during the meeting. He did feel a strange peace that everything would work out, but he had no earthly idea how. But he knew God had a heavenly idea, and that was all that was needed.

As the meeting time neared that afternoon, John Smith was the first to arrive. "What's this all about, Pastor?" Jerry explained this situation briefly, and said that he had no idea how this was going to work out. John asked to say a quick prayer, which Jerry was relieved to hear, but he was mainly relieved that John was not taking this badly. After John's simple prayer for peace, unity, and wisdom, however, Jerry understood why he had such a peace. God was clearly in control.

The other three class members arrived shortly, and, having been told that John would be attending, warmly greeted him, Jerry, and one another. Jerry opened the meeting with an informal prayer along the same lines that John had just prayed. Then he asked for anyone to jump in with a description of what had happened the night before that had precipitated this morning's visit to Mark. He explained that Mark had asked him to take this issue on because he did not feel qualified to handle it since it dealt with the controversial area of End Times theology.

John was the first to speak, with a smile and carefully chosen words. "Well, Mark is not alone in that. I am for sure not qualified to decide on End Times controversies either. I doubt even Pastor Jerry would want to take on that mantle."

"Of course not," responded Jerry, also smiling.

"But I fully understand Mark's reluctance to get involved. I guess I would like to hear from the others about their concerns, though, before I say anything else."

A few seconds of silence elapsed before the board member quickly recounted the teaching on the possibility of the Nephilim being involved in an End Times fulfillment of the Daniel passage. He did not mince words about the connotations of the phrase "they will mingle with the seed of men; but they will not adhere to one another." He admitted that neither he nor the others had even remembered that part of the prophecy, but that it seemed an unnecessary stretch to even bring up a fanciful interpretation of a minor Old Testament term that was not well understood. His concern, and he believed he spoke for the other two, and likely other class members, was that there are so many off-the-wall teachings about End Times that we need to stick to conservative principles of interpretation and not allow extra-biblical ideas to creep in. He quoted Paul's admonition to not give heed to fables and instead speak the things that are proper for sound doctrine (Titus 1:14, 2:1).

Jerry took a deep breath and was about to say something when John jumped in with an even tone, not taking his eyes off of the board member. "Joe, we've known each other for a long time. I really value your opinion, and I respect your command and understanding of the Word. I was trying to liven up the class with some unusual material, since I knew everyone was already familiar with the passage. I'm sorry if my reaching back to an obscure thought from Genesis seemed out of place. I don't give the idea much credence, either, but I thought the terminology was similar enough to at least invoke the possibility of scripture interpreting scripture. You have heard my teaching on how most of the references in the Gospels that relate Christ's coming to Old Testament passages would have been difficult to see from the Old Testament context. I guess I was pushing a remote possibility to illustrate that we cannot ever be completely sure about how a prophetic passage might be fulfilled. I should have explained why I took that approach, and I apologize that I didn't do that."

Joe likewise apologized that he and the others didn't bring up their concerns in the class, and that they took them to Mark without going to John first. John chuckled and explained that End Times prophecy always brings out the best in Christians, the best opportunities for misunderstanding, that is. Joe and the others laughed and agreed that they all needed to not take such speculations too seriously, and even have fun with them.

"Like one of the Pharisees said, we sure don't want to be found rejecting something that turns out to be true later on, just because it doesn't fit our idea of traditional, conservative interpretations." Jerry chimed in and wagged a finger at them in jest, saying that they'd better keep to their traditional, conservative interpretations in everything else besides End Times prophecy. They all said "Amen" to that.

After the group left, Jerry fell into his desk chair, relieved to turn his attention to his sermon notes that were behind schedule. He paused just a second before raising his laptop lid, and heard the Holy Spirit whisper, "Hey, Jerry. How do you think that went?"

"Oh, Lord. Yes, I meant to thank You for fixing everything so nicely."

"No, Jerry, that's not what I meant. What did you learn from that encounter?"

"Oh, well, I learned to trust in You to resolve dilemmas. I was surprised at how that worked. Especially having everyone in the same room and not having a speech prepared to pave the way."

"So how does this relate to your charge to feed your sheep organically?"

"What? Uh, oh, I hadn't even thought of that. Let me think. Organically. The church as a body, members of an organism. Well, I guess that shows that the members can work together to solve problems, that they have some natural capabilities to do that, and that as leaders we need to allow that process to work."

"Very good, Jerry. There's a little more. It's like the immune system of the body, like white blood cells dealing with an intruder, a potential infection. If the body is healthy, its members, even at the cellular level, can come together to intercept the intruder and easily contain and destroy it before it has a chance to do any further damage. What do you think would have happened if this hadn't been resolved quickly?"

"I suppose the class members would have continued to talk among themselves, get offended at the teacher, and eventually left the class and maybe even the church if they felt they weren't being heard and dealt with fairly."

"Yes, but your members were strong enough in the Word to know that they needed to bring this to leadership right away. It would have been better if they had gone directly to the teacher, even in class or right afterwards. It's always better to confront in love at the time of the perceived offense. Often people's motives are not what they seem to be, or they are quick to admit fault and apologize. In this case, however, I wanted you to see an example of how the simple teaching you are doing every Sunday is building up your local body and giving them the capabilities to deal with seemingly minor issues. But catching such minor items quickly is the key to keeping the body healthy and being strong enough to fight off more serious attacks later."

"Wow! I never thought of it quite that way. That gives me an idea for a very practical illustration for my sermon. Better get busy if I'm not going to offend the A/V department!"

"Go for it, Jerry! They would forgive you. But I think you'll be finished just in time."

# 18

## This Is It!

Two weeks later, as Jerry was preparing to leave the Green Room and join the worship that had just started for the second Sunday service, he heard a quiet voice whisper, "This is it." It was so real that he said out loud as he looked behind him, "What is it? Who said that?" Then he instantly realized it was the Holy Spirit, and he felt faith arise for an unusual move of God. He had feelings like this every now and then, but not with such a clear word, and not just before a service. He said a quick, "Amen, so be it, Lord Jesus!" and continued to his family's spot on the front row.

As the worship continued, Jerry found his eyes would not open as he focused on the character and glory of God. He felt God's love wash over him in slow, deep waves. Scriptures came to mind, accompanied by incidents that had happened over the past few months, from preparing for his sabbatical, to the miraculous encounters at the lake cabin, to the men's retreat and growth of effective small groups, to the working out of many revelations of God's grace and power, including reconciling with his family and understanding the organic relationships within the church body. He was overwhelmed by how much God had shown him and had accomplished through His church as he let go of preconceived ways of thinking and acting. As he allowed God to work freely in others without his usual attempts to control, even if with the best intentions, the circumstances and behaviors invariably worked out for the good. It had been a nervous but exhilarating time.

As the last strains of "This Is the Air I Breathe" drew to a close, Jerry, without thinking, took a deep breath. He pursed his lips and let it out, and realized that God had sovereignly filled his spirit with a fresh and abundant portion of the Holy Spirit. Jerry immediately fell to his knees, convulsing in tears. He then stretched out on the floor in the altar area and continued weeping. He heard the Lord say tenderly but firmly, "I have heard the cry of your heart and I am here to give you your deepest desires. I am filling this whole house with My Spirit, and it will never be the same. Prophesy, Jerry, prophesy from your spirit. Tell this house, My Body, My Bride, what I am saying and what is in your heart for them. Tell them about My love and your love for them. Tell them they were made to receive My love deep down, so deep that it heals their deepest wounds, their shame, and their disappointments. They never have to doubt My love for them again. They can go through the severest trials, the most sublime joys, and the monotonous routine of daily life, but they will always know My love and they will always trust in My Presence, even if they don't feel it. Jerry, tell them, tell them, tell them."

Jerry struggled to get to his knees, then to his feet, and made his way unsteadily up the steps to the pulpit. The order of service was far from his thoughts as he poured out God's words and his own heart for the next fifteen minutes. Then he collapsed once more and continued crying out to God through tears of joy and love for God's goodness. The worship team began playing familiar chords as the congregation sang spiritual songs in a heavenly language and harmony. This continued for another twenty minutes.

Jerry rose once again to the pulpit and spoke a simple message of repentance and coming to the Cross for God's love and forgiveness. He was speaking to himself as well as to the congregation. God's tangible Presence had sensitized him and everyone else to their need to get rid of every hint of pride, of bitterness, of anger, of fear and doubt, of jealously and covetousness. As he mentioned each area of sin, people all over the sanctuary cried out for forgiveness. Many sank back in their chairs or to their knees and wept tears of repentance and healing. Jerry continued to call on the power of God's infinite love to wash away every thought and feeling of shame as people were deeply pierced with remorse. Many felt such relief and joy flooding their souls that they laughed out loud and acknowledged God's forgiveness with shouts of gratitude and praise.

After another twenty minutes, Jerry remembered that this was the first Sunday of the month and Communion had been prepared. He shook his head in wonder at God's timing and provision. As he led the congregation in taking the bread and the juice, he summarized the lessons of the past few months that had found their way into his meditations and sermons on the church as an organic body. He reminded them that this was what Communion symbolized, the healed and unified body of Christ, appropriating God's forgiveness and extending forgiveness to others. How could we hold bitterness towards anyone knowing the price God paid with His blood to forgive them of their sins? And how could we feel unworthy or ashamed of ourselves knowing His boundless love was poured out at the Cross for us?

Jerry asked everyone, as they took the elements, to lay at Christ's feet any remaining feelings or thoughts that needed to be repented. He then asked them to picture themselves turning away, not looking back, but going straight to the empty tomb and gazing on Jesus' glory as He ascended to heaven and stands at the Father's right hand to pray for us and cheer us on. How can we not trust Him with everything in our lives, knowing He is interceding for us and encouraging us to walk in the grace and mercy that He has already purchased?

Jerry put down the juice container and stepped off the stage to join his wife and children on the front row. As he did, he asked everyone to gather with their family or with close friends, not leaving anyone by themselves, and end the service by praying for one another. He asked that God's Presence would go deep into each person's spirit and sustain them with faith and trust in the weeks and months ahead.

# 19

## Next Steps

Over the next few days, the church staff was buzzing about the service. Mark and Gabe met with Jerry the first thing Tuesday, after the ministers' day off on Monday.

"Pastor, Gabe and I have been talking. The whole church has been going wild on social media, as I'm sure you have seen. You have been strangely silent after what was clearly the most powerful service we've ever had. Is this the start of a revival? Should we be planning services during the week? What are you thinking?"

"Whoa, guys! Let's slow down. Yes, I know something special happened Sunday. Donna and I have talked about it a lot the last two days. Even the kids were impacted. Stephanie wants me to have a special service with the youth. Imagine that. She says her friends are ready to go deeper and want more of what we felt in that service. I've seen the Facebook and Twitter posts as well. I intentionally abstained, for a change, to see if others felt the same as I did."

"Well, what did you feel, Pastor?"

"I felt the same as you, Gabe. It was as much of the tangible Presence of God as I have ever felt. Very much like my times at the cabin last summer and this spring. It was even heavier because of the corporate setting, I'm sure. But just as personal, too. I truly believe we have reached a new level as a church body. Donna was surprisingly calm about it, but she said in no uncertain terms that this is a new thing, and that God is going to use us and this church in ways we have never imagined. What do you guys think God is up to? What is our next step?"

"Pastor, Gabe and I agree. This is a new thing for sure. I don't have any special insight, other than I know I am supposed to do whatever it takes to help sustain the atmosphere of repentance, personal holiness, and desire to know God more deeply. And for me personally, I believe He is saying to learn to feel His love for me and for others right in my gut. I have no problems thinking about God's love, but I felt things in the service that I didn't know were possible to feel. I felt the Father's love, just for a few minutes, in a gut-punching way. I mean, I almost hurt with a revelation of how much He wants to put in me and then do through me to touch others. I don't understand what that looks like in everyday life, but I want desperately to experience it."

"Gabe, what about you? You and your team flowed so beautifully Sunday. I know you had a profound experience."

"Yes, Pastor, I did. We all did. It seemed effortless. I listened to the recording yesterday, and I couldn't believe how the people were responding so well as we worshipped with new songs and harmonies. It was really heavenly. I have prayed about what comes next, but, like Mark, I'm all in with whatever direction you want this to go. I know you will hear and do the right thing."

"Well, thanks, guys. I have been praying, and I believe I have at least the next step. And I think it meshes with what I was seeing on social media over the last day and a half. I believe God wants us to do two things to sustain the new level we experienced Sunday. One is to have Sunday night "power" services. We tried that once a month a few years ago, but it was a lot of work, and seemed to just wear out the staff and minister mainly to the core members, but it never grew beyond that dedicated group."

"Yes, I saw that mentioned a few times, but it was before I came."

"Well, Gabe, it was fine, but when the building program started, we had other reasons for special activities and didn't want to stretch everyone too thin. Anyway, it's time to get back to that. I believe it would be similar with emphasis on worship songs, interspersed with short prayers, teachings, prophetic words, spiritual songs, and just waiting on the Holy Spirit's direction throughout. I don't think we need an order of service at all, and it's up to you how or if you want to plan the songs. Your team knows how to flow, so I am ok with not trying to plan much at all. I also want to make sure that you don't wear out yourself and the team. You might want to recruit some new folks and establish a rotation system so you don't have to lead every service."

"That's just what I was hoping, Pastor. We can do it. It will be exciting to have that kind of liberty."

"Mark, what do you think?"

"That sounds great. What about any announcements or offerings? Should we limit those, or just not plan on them at all?"

"Gabe?"

"Pastor, I think that's covered Sunday morning, so I don't see the need. But I'm curious how long the service would be."

"I was thinking we communicate an expectation of an hour, but then allow anyone who wants to hang around, perhaps at the altar area, to do so while the worship team continues softly for another 30 minutes or so. That will give people an opportunity to have their own private time to process what has happened during the day's services and to apply what they've heard to themselves."

"Sounds good. But you said two things. What else besides Sunday evening services?"

"I'll get to that, but I have one more thought on the Sunday evening services. I feel we should have one a month, maybe the last one, where we take Communion. This would replace the Sunday morning Communion. It would also be a link to Sunday's service that was so special. And it ties repentance at the Cross with the ongoing purpose of the church. It will help us stay grounded in the basics. I also plan to continue with the theme of the organic church. I feel we have just begun to understand that, and it will help provide continuity as well.

"OK, now for item two. I know this is going to sound strange, but I believe I am to start a series on Genesis and focus on the creation as God originally intended it. We will tie our 'revival' atmosphere to the goal of ushering in the restoration of God's design for our lives, our families, and for the church. By church, I mean our local church, as well as the Body and Bride of Christ."

"OK. I can already see some amazing song lists and a new stage design, Pastor."

"I knew I wouldn't have to say a word, Gabe!"

"OK, well I will definitely crank out some ideas for the small groups and adult education classes to complement the theme. And I'm sure the Oberlins will love to get the children and youth back to the basics. Everyone loves the Genesis stories."

"Thanks, Mark. And there's one more thing. I believe I am supposed to bring in a speaker on creation science."

"Really, Pastor? Uh, are you sure? You mean for a Wednesday night class?"

"No, Mark, I mean for a couple of Sunday services, and for a couple of youth services. I think we need to let our actions speak loudly. Our God is first of all the Creator, and if we are going to get serious about restoring that creation, we need to understand what the Bible says and how it is true about the most basic foundation of our faith. If we can't trust it in that area, how can we trust it anywhere? Isn't that what the world tells us, that the Bible is just a bunch of stories and illustrations that don't have much to do with the real world? If we are going to get really close to God, we have to embrace Him as our Father, but first as our Creator. It must be real to us, not just a story. It has to be eternal Truth. We have to be fully committed to His Word as the ultimate reality."

"OK, is this something you have studied? I don't recall you teaching on this."

"Actually, I haven't studied or taught on it at all. But I believe it is critical to laying a foundation for this 'revival' or whatever it is. I can't explain it. I just know it. I plan to study on it, of course, before I reach out to anyone, but I'm committed to do so."

"OK. I'll put feelers out for some options."

"Thanks, Mark. I feel strongly about this, as you can tell. I am actually kind of excited to get into an area that I've always been afraid of. God is going to have to show up on this one, because, believe me, I know how controversial it is. And I am ready to trust Him on it."

After Mark and Gabe left Jerry's office, he leaned back in his chair and whispered, "God, I hope You are in this big time. If we are going to launch out into the deep, I want to know You are right there, ready to pull us back into the boat if we become unsure or fearful. That may be a negative confession, but I'm just being real. OK, let's start making these changes and see what You have for us."

The rest of the week, Jerry saw a procession of staff, church members, and even other pastors who had heard about the Sunday service. He felt a strange peace about sharing his heart with each person, and even more peace about not worrying that he should be preparing for Sunday's services. He was determined to let the Holy Spirit lead him and provide just the right people and circumstances to prepare for the next steps. Sure enough, the Sunday morning and evening services were powerful, beyond even his expectations. The sanctuary was nearly full both services. God's Presence was strong, from the first worship song to the final benediction. The altar was packed with people repenting and asking for more of God's anointing.

As a result of many requests, Jerry added a second Sunday morning service. This was a full year earlier than he was expecting after having been in their new space less than two years. And the Sunday evening service was typically going two hours, and sometimes more. Far from being stretched by the additional services, the staff was invigorated and found that volunteers were increasing and were even more dedicated to helping with the logistics, nursery, and extra children's services. The Genesis series never got into the familiar stories of Abraham and his descendants, but the new insights into the creation passages and the Flood blew people away with God's awesome power and ultimate plans for redemption in spite of man's sinfulness.

The creation science lectures, as they could be best described, while a bit dry and fact-filled, gave the listeners a deep appreciation for God's infinite creativity, His incredible attention to details, and the overwhelming complexity of the physical creation. As the magnitude of these began to sink into everyone's mind, heart, and spirit, they understood, many for the first time, that they served a God who, indeed, could take care of their individual needs. No detail was too small, and no problem too complex for His loving attention. He was the ultimate Father, Creator, and Designer who worked all things together for their good.

In contrast, the speed and depth with which man pulled away and actively rebelled against God was more appalling than ever. Everyone recognized the urgent need for repentance at even the slightest tendency to have wandering thoughts. Many also came to the ongoing Tuesday night prayer services and used the personal prayer time after the short service to confess sin and ask for fresh baptisms with the Holy Spirit. The Wednesday night classes were filled to overflowing, and several new classes started up. The small groups were also impacted and became more personal versions of the Tuesday night prayer services. Jerry realized that, while they did not follow the model of nightly services as had many historical "revivals," many were in fact attending services of some kind most nights of the week.

After completing the Genesis Creation and Flood series, Jerry went back to the theme of the organic church. Especially after the creation science exposition of the life sciences, showing the amazing design and interdependent complexity of God's plant and animal kingdoms, Jerry was able to use numerous examples of how organisms complement one another and work together. The main "aha" for most of the congregation was the degree to which the complexity had obviously been lovingly designed.

The diversity and variation in purposes was seen to be infinitely rich, and yet each component was designed in such a way as to effortlessly play its part. There were even built-in corrective mechanisms when outside, potentially damaging influences, came into play. Jerry had fun exploring a whole new set of illustrations and applications, and even surprised himself at how insights from basic organic life principles could be meaningfully applied to the believer's walk.

Towards the end of the series on the organic church, Jerry asked the congregation to submit examples of other applications. He then used three of these during each of the last four weeks, making the point that we can all learn from one another. He encouraged everyone to realize that they have creative ideas to contribute, and that the body needs to hear from them. That is part of their purpose for which they were designed.

One of the surprise themes that was suggested multiple times was heaven and hell. One person in particular made an impassioned plea that these concepts were key teachings of Christ and would provide important motivation for the organic church's purpose, both from a negative and positive perspective. Jerry immediately saw that such a sermon series would perfectly complement the Creation theme. God created heaven on earth for Adam and Eve, but man's sin necessitated hell and the ark of Christ as God's redemptive answer. Revelation ultimately ties it all together and reveals the stunning role of the Millennium and Heaven on a restored Earth as God's ultimate destination for His redeemed Bride. Jerry touched on this at the end of the organic church series, but then followed with what would become his most popular series ever, titled "Heaven and Hell on Earth."

# 20

## Evaluating the Outpouring

After several more months with no apparent waning of enthusiasm by the congregation and many visitors from the city, state, and beyond, Jerry called his key staff and board together for an offsite one-day workshop on the Outpouring, as they had decided to call it. The goal was to evaluate what had been happening, good and bad, and to try to discern God's direction from this point on. Jerry had asked everyone to talk to their friends and a cross-section of attenders to get a feel for the people's attitudes. As he started the workshop, Jerry made it clear that he didn't want to hear a lot of self-congratulations. He wanted a real picture of how the staff and congregation were benefitting, but also any stress points or potential danger signs. He recounted several revivals or awakenings from the past few centuries and the factors that seemed to help or harm sustaining a move of God.

For example, the Moravian movement that started in 1727 was sustained for over a hundred years because of the emphasis on small groups devoted to prayer, accountability, and the basic Bible doctrines. Several of the awakenings were tied to a traveling evangelist that had an impact on large, diverse audiences, and then spread different forms of revival elsewhere. The main ongoing result was additional believers and churches being established, although not always with the same fire and growth. Several of the Pentecostal revivals waned after the inexperience and enthusiasm of a young leader led to congregational excesses, or obsessive, jealous, and other inappropriate behavior by leadership.

After the short, but sobering, history lesson, Jerry asked for feedback. Most felt that staying with the familiar meeting structure, with only the extra Sunday evening service, was a key to not wearing everyone out. It provided opportunity for those who wanted to attend more meetings to do so. The variety demonstrated that the Holy Spirit was fully at work in different settings and formats, from preaching and worship to teaching, prayer, and fellowship. The pattern set earlier in having a common theme across all of the meetings had served to maintain the thrust of the Outpouring and to ensure that changes in emphasis were permeating the entire church body and its ministries.

There were a few negatives at first, the main one being the amount of time required for staff to plan, prepare, and follow up with the increase in attendance, especially the children. The initial surge of volunteers had begun to dwindle. A few key people were being called on regularly and were showing signs of stress. Jerry asked for ideas on how to relieve this situation, and was surprised when the Oberlins suggested using paid workers in the children's ministry, particularly from the older youth. They had always been adamant about training dedicated volunteers to ensure a heart for ministry. But now they recognized that to keep the same ratio of workers that allowed the critical breakout discussion groups, they needed to attract more leaders from the youth.

They had experimented with paying a few workers and found that it caused a new level of consistency and excellence. The teenagers had all been touched by the Outpouring in the Sunday and youth services and were ready to share what they were feeling. With a nominal hourly payment, they were not only more open to additional training, but they also felt that the church valued their contribution, which they then took even more seriously. The adult leaders were able to focus on the main worship and teaching times and prepare the hearts of the children to be open in the discussion groups. As the youth leaders became more experienced, they were able to draw out the children to express their beliefs and questions and deepen their understanding of Biblical truths and their relationship with God.

Another negative had been the offerings. The growing number of visitors were simply not giving enough to offset the additional expenses. Jerry solved the situation with a short series on stewardship, emphasizing the need to give to the storehouse where you were being fed. He then kept the offering times very short and informal, so that visitors did not feel that was an emphasis. Mark said that had helped bring offerings in line with expenses. More recently the church was putting away a nice surplus every week. He mentioned that the board had entertained the idea of looking at the surplus as a kind of sinking fund should the Outpouring continue to grow attendance and perhaps require additional space and other improvements in the campus. That generated a lot of discussion and brainstorming. Jerry welcomed the ideas, but cautioned that it was too early to begin making serious plans.

The idea that had the most discussion was to start a school of ministry to formalize and expand on the principles of the organic church and the other teachings that had been instrumental in launching the Outpouring. George James suggested that it be structured in short term blocks of one or two weeks to accommodate the steady stream of serious visitors, many of whom were leaders and staff members at other churches across the state and the country. He did not think a school should become a permanent fixture, but rather a flexible vehicle for allowing those who could take a week or two off to soak in God's presence and go deeper in personal application. The emphasis would be on personal change, much like the experience Jerry had during his sabbatical and in the weeks afterward. You can't take others where you haven't been, he said two or three times, at least.

Jerry agreed wholeheartedly with George, and added that maybe it should not be called a school, but something to indicate a shorter learning cycle, like a seminar. He thought it could be modeled after the men's retreat the previous year, with two or three hours of teaching in the mornings, and then time the rest of the day to contemplate alone, discuss in small groups, work on mini-projects or papers, and have some fun and fellowship. The more he thought about it, he saw it also as an opportunity to develop leaders who would then facilitate the small groups and take part in the teaching at times, especially to give testimonies about the changes they had experienced in their personal lives.

At the end of the workshop, Jerry asked each person to name the main opportunity and the main threat they anticipated over the next few months. The overwhelming opportunity mentioned was to simply grow personally in deeper devotion and closeness to the Lord, and to rest in His provision for every aspect of their lives. There were two themes regarding threats. One was to not let the busyness and attention from outside parties distract the leadership from continuing to seek the leading of the Holy Spirit in services. The other threat they saw was from pride in thinking that their church was something special and deserved God's Presence because of all the effort being put into seeking Him. They never wanted to take Him for granted, and recognized that His tangible Presence in the services, and on the campus in general, was purely a sovereign act of grace.

Jerry ended the workshop with a prayer of thankfulness and joy for all God was doing in their midst. He echoed the idea that it was only His grace that sustained the Outpouring, and that they all needed His help in identifying areas where each of them should repent daily of any thoughts of self-sufficiency.

# 21

## The Seminars

Jerry and Mark had fun over the next few weeks planning for the Outpouring Seminars. They decided to have three versions for each of the several topics, a weekend format, a one-week format, and a two-week format. As the amount of work in putting these together became evident, they decided to hire a full-time pastor to direct the seminars and coordinate with the growing adult classes on Wednesday nights. Some of the Wednesday night classes effectively became a fourth format based on the seminars, with an hour and a half class weekly for twelve weeks. One of the goals was to capture the seminar teachings on video for use during the weekly classes, and then eventually make them available to other churches, along with workbooks and facilitator guides.

After interviewing several candidates, they picked Johnny Johnson, a fairly new church member who had recently graduated from a Bible school. He had been a trainer in a corporate HR department and was thrilled to be able to use his skills in course development and presentation, as well as his theology training. Johnny had been in the initial service when the Outpouring began, and was intimately familiar with all of Jerry's teachings. His wife, Joanna, was a middle school English teacher, and eagerly volunteered to help compile and edit the curriculum and teaching materials.

The Outpouring Seminars quickly became well known and respected in the community. Jerry and Johnny were careful to meet with other area pastors to assure them that they were not trying to poach other church members. At the suggestion of the pastor of the largest church in the area, who fully supported the Outpouring and had attended several services himself, they made the teaching materials available to the other churches at a deep discount, and conducted "train-the-trainer" sessions for experienced teachers who could adapt the concepts to their own congregations. Jerry made a point of saying publicly that the church did not want to profit at the expense of others, but just wanted to be able to fund the additional staffing and expenses that the Seminars incurred, especially production of the videos.

Some of the other churches in the area, especially those not open to the Pentecostal, Holy Spirit-led aspects of the Outpouring, discouraged their members from participating in any of the services or seminars. This, of course, piqued the curiosity of some, who not only investigated, but decided to move permanently. Jerry tried at first to discourage such movement, but after being shunned by a few area pastors, he reluctantly decided to let the chips fall where they may. He prayed that the Holy Spirit would work in those churches, and especially in their pastors, to bring about unity in the Body of Christ. He began a personal study on the organic church at large. He focused on how individual churches could see themselves as fitting together without having to agree on details, even those areas that seemed doctrinally important. He was inspired by Count Zinzendorf and the Moravian prayer movement, where the Count learned to focus on the areas of agreement and allow respectful freedom regarding differences.

Jerry did not apologize for the importance and emphasis on the role of the Holy Spirit and the gifts of the Spirit in energizing the Outpouring, but he suggested to skeptical pastors that they at least review some of the teaching materials, which he provided at no cost. After he completed his study of the organic church at large, he provided that teaching also at no cost, and even conducted workshops specifically for other church pastors. Most, after reading or attending these workshops, were open to their members investigating what was happening, if nothing other than to not push them away by forbidding it.

Jerry's teaching on the organic church at large had an even bigger impact on his congregation. Most who had been in the Pentecostal tradition for a while dismissed the mainline evangelical churches as being closed-minded about the Holy Spirit and severely limited in their ability to serve God's purposes. However, Jerry's teaching emphasized the great differences in function of the various members of an organism. By nature, it was not likely, nor expected, that such differences could be resolved. They are, by design, different! He challenged those who thought they had more revelation and knowledge than their brothers in Christ to recognize that attitude as pride and to repent quickly and walk in humility of thought and speech towards them.

He gave examples of traditional denominations who were strong in their memorization of the Word and application of sound Bible principles, especially in ministering to the lost and disadvantaged. Who are we to judge their heart or their contribution to the kingdom? Doesn't judgment start in our own house? Are we walking in full obedience to everything we already know? Can we afford to criticize others when we are so easily distracted by the cares of this life? Isn't our most effective witness that of a changed life? If we believe in the power of the Spirit, are we being led by, and exhibiting, that power in everyday circumstances?

Jerry's teachings on the organic church at large were being accepted slowly but steadily. As a result, he had to increase the frequency of his workshops for pastors. He found that they were attending at the suggestion of their colleagues and church members, and were therefore more open to the new paradigms Jerry was presenting. One of the biggest "ahas" many pastors were having was the idea that they could depend on the Holy Spirit, or God, if that was the way they saw it, to create circumstances and put people around them who were intentionally designed to bring out new and better ways of thinking and acting. In other words, the idea of God working all things together for our good seemed much more practical and pervasive than they could imagine.

Jerry taught that every detail of our life can be seen as furthering His purpose for us if we will accept this principle and actively engage our mind, our hearts, and our spirits to seek out what our response should be. This is actually a form of praying without ceasing that becomes a natural part of our life. And we don't have to get super spiritual about "hearing a word" before doing anything. We can depend, in faith, on God to hear our minute by minute "prayers" and then orchestrate our environment to lead us in the next optimal step. Our steps will be ordered by Him as we seek Him in trust. Sure, there are times when He will speak in our inner spirit, but we don't have to stress about hearing every detail of every situation. We can truly rest in His provision.

To illustrate these principles, Jerry had most of the workshop groups do an exercise that he had discovered after his sabbatical in writing out a short sermon without preconceived ideas or a logical outline or format. It was a very practical exercise, resulting in something most of them would use, but also that might challenge them to launch out in faith way beyond their comfort zone. It never failed that almost every participant was shocked and gratified at how the Holy Spirit moved through them as they simply rested and trusted without reservation or expectation.

This single experience convinced even the most hardened skeptics that their God was bigger than they thought, and that they could depend on Him to take them places, in their own churches, that they never dreamed possible. One non-charismatic pastor took the exercise seriously. He started writing immediately after a quick prayer of guidance and was shocked that he found his words leading him to build up to an altar call for physical and emotional healing. He never wavered, however, and reported back to Jerry that the service was a turning point in his church. They started a prayer chain and had regular evening services specifically for healing, with many testimonies of documented results.

# 22

# Family Tensions

Jerry had just finished his fifth Friday-Saturday weekend Outpouring Seminar. The pastors and leaders of several churches in the state, and even from nearby states, were off to their hotels for dinner and much-needed sleep before attending the Sunday services. Jerry conducted the Friday morning introduction and Saturday evening close, and a couple of other sessions each day. By Saturday evening he was exhausted, but in a good way. He knew the Holy Spirit would refresh him as he slept, and that He would guide him in the Sunday services. He wearily unlocked and opened his front door after parking in the driveway. Donna met him in the entryway and said quietly, "Jerry, we need to talk." The kids were at a special youth event, and she wasn't smiling.

"What's the matter?"

"I know you're tired, dear, but I need to share some things with you."

"OK. Let me get a glass of iced tea, and let's sit on the patio."

Jerry knew this was going to be a significant conversation, so he lingered in the kitchen and shot up a quick prayer. "God, help me be sensitive to my wife. You know I'm tired, so give me energy to focus on her tonight." He joined Donna on the patio, and sat down beside her saying, "What's on your mind, honey?"

"Jerry, the last year has been incredible, hasn't it?"

"Yes, life-changing, exciting, challenging, and at times frustrating. For all of us."

"Well, that's what I want to talk about. The frustrating part."

"OK. What in particular?"

"Oh, not any single thing. Just a lot of little things. Obvious things like the amount of time and energy we, you especially, have been spending at the church, ministering, studying, praying. All good things."

"But?"

"But, don't you feel it has taken a toll on our family? On our relationship?"

"Yes, that's why we have purposed to have our weekly date nights. Have you not enjoyed those?"

"Of course, but even during those precious times we talk mostly about the church and the latest things happening in the Outpouring. I love to see and talk about what God is doing in the church, but I also want to feel that we are growing together, closer to one another, and as a family."

"Gosh, I feel that we have done that. I have a whole new understanding and respect for you and the kids as a result of the insight about the organic church and family. I really try to see your needs and suggestions as part of God's guidance for my life. It's even got me to listen more deeply to Steve, and Don, and Stephanie. I believe their reactions and struggles to become their own identities have helped me see how we all have to deal with these issues of pride versus faith and confidence. It's a tough battle to believe I can do all things through Christ who strengthens me, and at the same time humble myself and give preference to others. How do I fulfill my dreams and what I believe God has called me to do while giving in to the demands and needs of others? I know these things work together, but they pull at our hearts and minds, and I see the tension in our family as an up close and personal example of what the church body is going through."

"Well, that sounds good, but don't you see how quickly you turn the conversation about us into a sermon illustration? Sorry if that sounds blunt, but that's what I'm talking about. I feel like I am living in a fishbowl and everyone sees us, and our family, as a continuing object lesson. Sometimes I just want to go away and live on a deserted island so we can get real about our own thoughts and feelings without having to think about how it affects everyone else. I just want to know and love the real you. And I want the same for our kids. Our relationships are going on into eternity, and I don't want to have regrets about what we did with them these few years on earth."

"OK. You accuse me of being super-spiritual, but isn't that what you're doing? I mean, bringing up eternal relationships, and all. Really? I'm trying as best as I know how to balance all of these needs. A growing church, a significant revival—these are important to a lot of people, to their eternal destiny, if you want to use those terms. I know it's been hard on you and the kids, but I've done all I know to do, and now I'm not feeling your support like I used to. What's going on?

Donna stared evenly into Jerry's eyes and without hesitation continued, "What's going on is a broken relationship. You think you have to balance me, your wife, and your children with anything else? Haven't you always said that a pastor's first priority is his family? What has changed? Is God not able to continue the Outpouring without you having to be involved in every weekend seminar? Are you really so important? It makes me sick to think that we have come this far to see you get so distracted with wanting to share God's glory. Isn't that what you are doing?"

Jerry let Donna's words sink in and knew he didn't need to respond right away. He thought about the weekend encounter he had almost a year ago to look deep into himself about what was causing strained relationships with her and the kids. Had he let his heart wander from the powerful lessons he had learned about not trying to control his own life? About how that had turned into controlling his family? He looked directly into her eyes for a while and said softly, "Honey, what you are saying hurts, but I have to admit that you are so right on. None of this church stuff, organic or otherwise, revival or Outpouring, is as important as our relationship and our family. I am so sorry I have lost sight of that. And I am even more appalled that I have hurt you so deeply. And the kids. What do you think we need to do to fix it?"

Donna wasn't expecting such a quick and affirmative recognition, but she had been thinking about how to improve. "I am grateful that you see what's going on. I really am. I hate to say that I expected this to be a big deal. But if you really want to fix things, I do have a suggestion."

"I want to hear all about it."

"Well, I would like for us to have a family sabbatical."

"You mean, a nice vacation, like the one a couple of years ago at the camping resort?"

"No, I mean a real sabbatical, like the one you took just after that vacation. I have to admit that I was quite jealous of your time at the cabin and the breakthroughs you had with some of the church leaders. It led to tremendous breakthroughs for us as well as the whole church, and has had an impact on many others outside our circle. But why shouldn't we have that kind of experience with each other, and with our children? You've always said the family was God's first institution, long before there was a church. And you have really tried to keep those priorities, I know. I just think if we are going to go to the next level, we need to do something different. And a sabbatical, or something like it, is the first thing that came to mind as I have been praying about this. So, what do you think?"

"Wow. What a great idea! I'm excited just thinking about it. What would a family sabbatical look like? I don't think I've ever heard of anyone intentionally doing that."

"I know. I tried not to think too much about the details, because I want it to be something we work out together, and with the kids. Kind of like the camping vacation, but this time different. For sure, I don't plan to do any cooking! I guess the only thought I have is that part of it would be just for us, and part with the kids. I think it's mainly about spending time together, but, like your cabin experience, I want to be open to what God might do beyond our expectations."

"So, as you are talking, I am seeing something. I see two weeks for us and two weeks with the kids. The key is to not plan too much activity, but rather pick a place where we can have a combination of privacy in a beautiful setting, along with access to entertainment, restaurants, and shopping, if we want."

"Yes, that's what I'm talking about! Seriously, honey, that sounds wonderful. Especially the part about not planning activities. It should be a time to rest and connect with one another. Our lives are so hectic, especially this last year. We need a break as well as a breakthrough!"

"OK. Let's pray right now and see what ideas God gives us."

With the children's input, Donna and Jerry designed a low-key, inexpensive, but fun and relaxing vacation, as they chose to call it. They did not want to make this sound too spiritual, and they separated the two, two-week periods in the summer so they wouldn't cause scheduling problems for Jerry and the church. The board was more than happy with Jerry's request, especially since he had not taken any days off since the Outpouring began.

Jerry was tempted, just for a minute, to make his family's decision an example for the church and suggest that they suspend the regular Outpouring schedule for the summer. He quickly dismissed the idea, keeping with Donna's concerns about his family always being an object lesson. However, without his even mentioning it, the topic was raised at the next executive staff meeting. Mark, Gabe, and Johnny had been talking about a summer break of sorts and had come up with a way to give the staff some relief without diminishing the continuity of the Outpouring sessions. Jerry was grateful and inwardly amazed at God's grace in working through staff and congregation to provide a time of refreshing without anyone having to feel guilty that they were backing off the commitment to maintain the move of God.

# 23

## The Family Sabbatical

Jerry's family sabbatical was more restful, and yet more fruitful, than he could have imagined. He intentionally held back on trying to generate opportunities for meaningful interaction with the children, and even with Donna. As a result, no one felt pressure to have serious discussions, but after hearing the stories of Jerry's cabin encounters, and after the year of Outpouring, everyone just naturally brought up deeper issues than they had ever done in a family setting. Steve had latched on to the creation science and organic body analogy teachings, and had lots of questions and opinions. Jerry was amazed at his depth of understanding and the research he had done. Don had witnessed several unexplainable healings of serious physical problems among his friends, and had become interested in intercessory prayer as a means to see more such supernatural interventions. He had picked up a book about this to read over the summer and was full of questions and ideas. Jerry sensed that Don was making a major commitment to the things of God, and relished the idea of mentoring him along his journey. Stephanie and Donna had been asked to teach one of the Outpouring Seminar sessions on dealing with teenagers, first from the teenager's perspective and then from the parent's perspective. It had become one of the most popular topics, and they were both eager to get feedback and examples from Don and Steve as they were going through typical changes and issues.

Jerry was amused that his family had turned into such spiritual nerds, so he made sure they also had lots of play time and unusual experiences.

They stayed in two different areas with the kids, one week in a rustic dude ranch, and the second week at a nice resort-style hotel near a large shopping and entertainment center. As if those weren't enough, during Jerry and Donna's adult vacation, the kids went to high-adventure camps one week, and then spent the final week with the families of their best friends.

    Jerry and Donna found an inexpensive rural B&B where they spent hours walking shaded trails, reading on a balcony overlooking a beautiful valley, and eating a variety of home cooking in the surrounding small towns. The best part was the undivided attention they were able to give one another. Donna had gotten a marriage counseling manual from a local pastor who specialized in such sessions. She thought some of the exercises would provide interesting questions to consider if they were having trouble filling the hours together. Jerry at first rolled his eyes when she brought the manual out, but after flipping through it, he realized that they truly had not had deep conversations about many of the topics. He actually had no idea what Donna liked or thought about a lot of things. He decided to tackle this head on and shocked her with his intense commitment to complete many of the chapters together. They were both a bit ashamed at not having intentionally discussed topics such as in-law issues, and they creatively changed some of the topics to apply to "after years" of marriage rather than pre- and early marriage. Needless to say, the increased intimacy they experienced in conversation translated to increased intimacy in other areas. While they enjoyed the experience greatly, they made a pact to not share any of what they had done or learned with the church for at least a year. Then, if it continued to bear fruit, they would definitely look at designing a long weekend marriage encounter like nothing else they had seen.

# 24

## The First Year and Beyond

As the summer grew to a close, the pastors and board had a one-day workshop to review the first year of the Outpouring and discuss the next year. In general, the pastors felt that the lower impact schedule during the summer was greatly appreciated by volunteers and staff alike, but they had the sense that they were marking time. The Outpouring had continued on an even keel, but that very consistency almost raised expectations that something new was coming, a shift of some kind. Jerry led the group in a prayer of thanksgiving for the past year's fruit and the blessings so many had enjoyed. Then he shifted into a prayer of dedication, to be willing to lay everything down, even their expectations of what might be coming. "Lord, we just want to hear from You, to see what You are doing in heaven, and then to bring that to our circumstances here and now. What would You have us do? Who would You have us be?"

After a few minutes of whispered and not-so-whispered prayers, the room got quiet. Finally, Janet, the prayer pastor, spoke, first softly, and then in increasing volume. "I believe the Holy Spirit is speaking to us very gently. He is wooing us and drawing us to the Father, through the grace of His Son, who has paid the price that we might live in the fullness of the Spirit. And that is His word for us today, and for the next few days and weeks and months—that we would continue to grow and live in the fullness of the Spirit. We are never to lose the sense of His Presence that we have felt this past year. We are to cherish it and expect it, yes, and desperately seek it if it seems far away at times. He is not far away, but He wants us to draw near when it seems that way, and then He will meet us in our hour of need. This is to become not just a style of worship as a body, but a lifestyle for each individual. We must each seek His divine favor and His gifts and His purpose for now, for the next stage in our life, and for eternity. Now, Father, we do seek You. We seek Your will, and ask that it might be done on earth as we know it is being done in heaven at this very moment. Fill us now. Fill us moment by moment and day by day with Your precious Holy Spirit. We fall before You and adore You."

Gabe began to sing "This Is the Air I Breathe" and was soon joined by everyone in the room. As the last strains faded away, Jerry changed the atmosphere with a strong plea, "God, our Father, in Jesus' mighty Name, we fall before You in repentance. We do not presume that Your favor is in any way because of what we have done. We know that, but for Your grace, we would not be able to stand before the evil one and his minions. We would give in to his weakest lies and deceptions. We have no good thing in us except our dependence on You for our very breath. Now we come before You, not in our own strength, but only at Your command, humbly, and with full recognition that we are nothing without You. Hear our cries and give us wisdom for this next stage, individually, as families, and as a church body. We are Your servants. We humbly repent before You as we wait on Your grace."

Gabe picked back up with the chorus, and each person, with various intensities, cried out in repentance for negative attitudes and words, and for actions committed and omitted. For the next twenty minutes, all were on their knees or on their faces in sorrow and repentance. Then one by one they began to stand up, lift their arms heavenward, and praise God for hearing their prayers and pouring out His mercy and grace. Gabe ended with "You're a Good, Good Father," and everyone took their seats in an attitude of expectation.

Jerry stood up and addressed the meeting quietly. "I believe I have a word from the Lord that complements Janet's. His Presence has been so real today, and I hear Him speaking encouragement and presenting a challenge. He is encouraging us to continue to seek Him diligently in our gatherings, whether on Sundays or during the week, at church or in our homes, at work or at play. He is always near to us and wants us to stay close to Him. He is just a breath away. Even the shortest, simplest, quietest prayer He will hear and take to heart. But it's up to us to voice it, out loud, with a whisper, or just in our thoughts. He will hear and answer. More so that we can imagine, He delights to give good things to His children who come to Him in faith.

"But He also has a challenge for us. We are in danger of taking His Presence for granted. And there is a very short distance between that and pride. We cannot let complacency take root. We can choose to move on into a deeper relationship with Him, or He can orchestrate circumstances that will provide that motivation. It's like we've learned about judgment. It is better to judge ourselves now than to think we are doing well and suffer loss later when He confronts us at the Judgment Seat of Christ. Likewise, it is better for us to shake off even the slightest hint of complacency and determine how we should move on into deeper levels of intimacy and knowledge of Him.

"Here's what I believe we are to do over the next few minutes, or hours, or whatever it takes. I would like a volunteer to take detailed notes on what everyone says. OK, Mary, thanks for that. You have a gift for listening and recording. This will be one of the most important things you ever do. And don't hesitate to speak up, yourself. Now, I believe we are to simply brainstorm ways we, individually, as well as a body, can take what has happened in the last year and build on it to see new levels of relationships with the Lord and with one another. That's it. Who's first?"

Mark jumped in unapologetically, "I have been thinking about this all week. I have sensed within myself the beginnings of complacency, and it has really bothered me. I didn't know what it meant or what to do about it until just now. I don't know about anyone else, but I believe I need to soak deeply in the Word, especially Psalms, the Prophets, the Gospels, and Revelation. These come straight from God's heart, and I want to saturate my soul, not just my mind, with them. I'm going to resist having a schedule or using commentaries. I want this to be a personal journey that goes deep and takes as long as it takes to get hold of my heart. OK, I'm done."

"Wow, Mark! That was short, sweet, and powerful. I am feeling convicted about doing the same thing. Can't wait to see what happens in both of us. Who's next? Mary?"

"Yes, Pastor, I'll type this out later, but I can't wait to say it. I have to admit that I, like many of my children's workers and volunteers, have not been as fully engaged in the Outpouring as I would like to have been. We are having an impact on the children, and we are seeing incredible growth in most of them. But it has taken a lot of preparation and effort, emotionally and physically. Frankly, I am drained. I feel close to God and I depend on Him for inspiration and words of encouragement for the kids, but I have had a number of personal and family crises, as most of you know. My mother's illness, coupled with our daughter's disabilities, have taken a toll. I have been praying all year, but feel like I'm hitting a stone ceiling.

"Just now, however, the Holy Spirit has been speaking to me that this has been a test of my persistence, and that He has provided the grace to get through this difficult time. I don't know how it is going to work out, but I believe that a time of refreshing is about to begin. Just hearing that word is refreshing and encouraging to me. I am trusting God to fulfill this promise, as He has so many times in the past. And I trust that He will also give Tom and me a strategy for making up what we have missed out on this past year. Well, I'll shut up and start typing. That's what I know, and I'm tired but excited to see how it is going to be fulfilled."

"Mary, you won't believe what I am about to tell you. Don't type for a few more minutes, trust me. I was going to wait until later today to tell you and Tom this, but a group of your volunteers has been meeting the past few weeks on this very topic. They presented a proposal to the church board last week, and I am happy to tell you that it was approved. You and Tom are being given a sabbatical of your own. It is for two weeks, in addition to your normal vacation, to be taken in one chunk. In addition, we are granting you $5,000 to spend any way you want. We encourage you to spend it on yourselves during the sabbatical period. As you know, Donna and I just finished such a sabbatical, and it was fantastic. I can't wait to hear your and Tom's report!"

"Pastor, I don't know what to say. I know how meaningful the sabbatical you took and then you and Donna enjoyed more recently. Tom and I have talked about what we would do if we ever had that luxury. So we know exactly how this is going to work out now! I am so excited. And you won't believe it, but a big part of our dream is to spend quality time with one another and with the Lord. This is just what we need to be refreshed in all ways. Thank you and the board so much. I will find out who those volunteers are and thank them personally! And most of all, thank God for His faithfulness!"

Gabe was the next to speak. "Pastor, everyone, I have a serious confession to make. No, really. The Outpouring has been amazing for me and my team. It's like the ultimate dream for a worship leader to be in a true revival and flow with the Holy Spirit in new and exciting ways. But I have to admit that there are some things I haven't handled very well. Let me put that another way. I have been guilty of pride and deceit against this ministry and against God. Before you say anything, let me continue.

"As you all know, we have used several of the songs I have written during the Outpouring, and our first album has brought in quite a bit of revenue. Many people have responded on our social media about how much it has meant to them, and I have heard personally from a number of worship leaders in other churches throughout the country that they are using our music and seeing much fruit. That's all well and good, even wonderful. But there's a problem. As this group also knows, I personally receive 50% of the royalties for the songs I've written that are sold or used by others. The unexpected extra money these past six months has really blessed my family at a time when we've had significant needs.

"So, as we have been planning the second album, I found it very tempting to include even more of my songs. We are about to start the production cycle on our live recordings and studio re-recordings. But recently I saw that I have not been doing what is right. There are other songs that have had more impact in our worship times the past few months that I have neglected to consider for the album. That is just not right, and I feel the Holy Spirit convicting me of pride and greed. So I repent before you and this group. I am going to rework the tracks we have already laid down, and will replace three of my songs with the ones that should be on the album. I am so sorry that I let this happen. And I am also doubling my tithe on the royalties that I receive for this second album. Please forgive me."

The room was silent for what seemed like a full minute. Finally, Jerry spoke with a low voice, full of compassion. "Gabe, I know the struggles you have had financially, and I have been praying for breakthrough. I believe that your sensitivity to the Holy Spirit's conviction is a turning point, and that God will truly pour out a blessing on you that you would not have believed possible. So, I'm sure I speak on behalf of this group when I say I forgive you. May your creativity and intimacy with God increase and bear much fruit for this Outpouring, and for many years to come."

There were several other affirmations of Gabe. Then George James stood up and cleared his throat. "Gabe, I admire your willingness to be transparent and say tough things in front of this whole group. But I have to ask you to forgive me. As the Outpouring has gone on for longer than I ever expected, I have found myself growing a bit tired and taking things for granted, in spite of knowing better. Quite frankly, the length and intensity of the praise and worship has been a challenge. I have found myself, and therefore my wife, coming in late, especially for the Sunday evening celebrations. I have been feeling distracted and a bit out of it lately, and I now see why. It's the trite phrase, 'What it takes to get it, it takes to keep it.' I have lived by that in my professional life, but I have let my guard down lately in church matters, and I have paid a steep price. I have knowingly sinned, against you, against Pastor, and against God. Please forgive me, Gabe, and you all."

Jerry stood up quickly. "Okay. Now I have to confess my sin as well. Gabe, like George, I have been guilty of coming in late during praise time, and sometimes not until the transition time, especially during the second service. At first I made the excuse that I needed to rest my voice and that the standing was bothering me. But really, I was just wanting to relax and veg out. As George said, the intensity was getting to be so heavy that I couldn't sustain it physically or emotionally. At least that's what I thought. Just now, though, I am reminded of the passage that it is not by my strength but by His Spirit that He sustains and encourages me. It is exactly in my weakness that His strength is able to come through.

"I know these things and have tried to practice them in the tough times, as many of you know. But during the amazingly good time recently, I have let down my guard. The devil will attack us from all sides, and I should have not been fooled by this obvious ploy. Well, like Paul, the closer I get to God, the more I realize how far I have to go. It is refreshing to know that I have more opportunities in this life, and then in eternity, to learn and grow and please Him. And, Gabe, I'm going to start by being the most enthusiastic worshipper on the front row. And in this church that is going to be tough to do!"

Gabe just smiled and said, "I love you, Pastor Jerry."

Bob Newcomb had been very quiet during the session. After a short pause he spoke slowly and carefully, "Guys, and ladies, this is not at all like me, but I believe I have a word from the Lord. I assume it applies to where we are going with the Outpouring, but I leave that to you all. The word is this, that we are to delve deeper into the meaning of the organic church and the organic nature of this last year's movement of the Holy Spirit. I don't know any details, but I sense that we have just scratched the surface of what God has for us. I am hearing that we have done well, and that we have doubled our unity as a body, but that we have gone from five percent to just ten percent of where we could be at this time. This is not a negative, but rather a challenge to grow deeper in our relationships with one another and with the Lord.

"I have followed Pastor's teachings on this and done additional study on my own. I was feeling pretty good about where we are and how far we have come, but I am compelled to say by the Spirit that there is more, much more. I humble myself before this word and before you all. I do not have answers. I have fought for a couple of hours about even saying this, but I could not hold it in any longer. So someone help me out. Tell me I'm out of line, and I will gladly repent of my foolishness, or tell me what's next and I will gladly jump on board."

"Bob, as you are talking, I am definitely feeling a witness in my spirit. I know you are hearing from the Lord, and I know it is the most important thing we have yet to discuss. However, I am not hearing anything specific, either. When that happens, I fall back to my wife. Donna, do you have any insight on this? I don't mean to put you on the spot, but I feel prompted to ask. If you have something, take your liberty and tell us."

"Well, I have had a thought stirring inside of me for most of the day. It seems so odd, but I will take this as a sign to put it out there for discussion. It actually does have to do with the idea of the organic church. We have gone into the analogy of the biological organism, and how the various parts work together under the leadership of Christ as the head. But I think it does go deeper, and starts at an even more fundamental level within our individual beings, within our body, soul, and spirit. We each are so complex, designed by the Master in His image, with a body made up of various organisms and organs, a soul made up of different elements, the mind, will, and emotions, and then a spirit, which I certainly don't understand, that somehow communicates with God's Holy Spirit.

"This all boggles my mind. I'm sure God created all of these parts to work in perfect harmony, but then sin entered in and created division and disunity, between man and God, between man and woman and other men, but also between the parts of a man. We are to love God and others as we love ourselves. We tend to focus on loving God and others, but our ability to do that depends on being able to love ourselves. This is the message I have been burdened with. Loving myself. Getting all the parts of myself aligned, organically, so that I am functioning the way I was originally designed.

"I truly believe that this is the missing piece to organic relationships. We have to be whole within ourselves. I think that this process begins with our salvation. We have to have God's Spirit working through our spirit to transform it, then our mind, will, and emotions. Only then we can have faith to be whole in our body. I want to be a member of Christ's church, His body, but I need to be whole myself to be of much use to the local body and then the body at large. OK, I've said it. I'll shut up. I am not a teacher or a pastor, but you asked, and I am not shy about sharing my feelings."

"Wow. I think that's it, Donna. Anyone else have a thought on this? Gabe?"

"Yes, Pastor, I do. That's really what was at the bottom of my confession just now. I was feeling dirty, not liking myself, just as Donna brought out. And as Bob said, I felt that I had to get that right before I could go on, you know, to another level. I know repentance is key. And I mean the kind that comes from a lot of effort in prayer, and a lot of patience in hearing from the Holy Spirit. When it's something that strikes at the core of your being, you simply can't see it yourself. It takes the light of the Word, both the logos and rhema Word, to shine in those dark places that we don't want to go, and that we don't even realize are there. In my case, it came from reading Psalm 91:1 about dwelling in the secret place of the Most High. That was my prayer during a time of fasting, and I sought that place diligently. That's when I realized my sin. In that place, there is no room for selfish pride or anything else but love for Him. I wanted it so much that I had to acknowledge and repent of my sin.

"That just happened a few days ago, and I haven't been the same since. I truly believe, as much as is possible at this point in my life, that I am dwelling in that secret place. I feel His Presence and love to a degree that I have never experienced before. I believe that is what Donna is saying. It's not just a matter of introspection and rooting out evil thoughts and behaviors. That comes, but it's first about desiring above all to dwell in the secret place of the Most High. He then hides us and protects us from the enemies of our soul, whether man or demonic spirits, or our own insecurities and doubts leading to self-rejection.

"The rest of that Psalm, and many other Psalms, are the Psalmist crying out for deliverance from his enemies, and seeking to purify his own soul from guilt and fear. The ultimate answer, over and over, is to trust in the Almighty. That, I believe, is the simple, but profound, secret. We have been hearing it and applying it the past year or two, and I think the next step is to live it day by day, minute by minute, dwelling in His glorious Presence.

"In that place, or I should say, this place, there is no room for sinful thoughts. You sense them as soon as the devil tries to plant them in your mind. They never make it into your feelings or actions or words. You immediately replace them with love for Christ and what He has done for you so that you know that He loves you and has provided for your daily deliverance. It's great! Like our theme song for the Outpouring, it's the air we breathe, minute by minute. In this atmosphere, we truly can be whole. Not perfect, but knowing that our Father loves us and gives us everything we need to be victorious over sin and death. And to bring that same life to others."

"Wow, Gabe, that's awesome. I know that has been a tough journey. I don't know anyone more sensitive to the Holy Spirit, except Donna, of course. You have shown us that no matter how far we think we've come, God wants to refine us and draw us even closer. All we have to do is recognize that next level of repentance, and then He will lead us into the next level of intimacy.

"And the idea of really feeling His Presence minute by minute, that is so hard, and yet so necessary. I think I'm there at times, and it never fails that I get distracted with something totally unexpected. Then it's hours before I even realize that I have been operating in my own strength. Sure, He trusts us to figure out things on our own and make decisions on our own, but that only works if we are constantly aware of His Spirit living in us and confirming our motives, decisions, and actions. That's how we learn, by stepping out in faith to do things we don't feel qualified to do, and then recognizing the affirmation of the Spirit. As we experience that day after day, we learn to rest in it. That builds our faith to go even deeper. The challenge is to see even distractions as opportunities to continue to operate in that rest, and to not allow our emotions or our logical thought processes to override what we know in our hearts is the right thing to say or do."

"OK, Pastor. Then how does all of this translate to the church as a whole? Do we each have to figure this out on our own? Is there something else we can do as leaders to prepare our body to walk in this constant awareness? I suppose it's really all about obeying and loving in all things, right?"

"Yes, George. That's the bottom line. It's easy to say and teach about, but we all know it's another thing completely to do it. I think as we go deeper ourselves, each one of us individually, the relationships we have already begun to build on will be just that much richer. We will encourage one another to grow in this way individually. The question is whether we can make changes in our services, and our small group and education programs, to help this growth process along. What do you all think?"

Donna was the first to speak. "Well, Jerry, as far as the main services, your preaching, that is, I think you have laid a wonderful foundation and have touched on a lot of these principles already. I know you don't like to do it, and that's why I'm saying it in front of this group, but I think you should be more personal and vulnerable about how you are walking this inner journey yourself. It's more comfortable to illustrate principles with examples of outward behaviors, but when it comes to our inner motivations and feelings, it's hard. You think others can't identify with your specific situation, especially being a pastor.

"I think you'd be surprised at how many of us have the same doubts and frustrations at wanting to do and think what is right, but constantly coming up short. We need to know that that's all right, and that the main thing is to keep at it. Stay in the ring, as we've learned in our marriage and other close relationships. You have to treat yourself the same way. Believe the best about yourself, don't give the devil even a toehold of doubt about your intentions. But also don't beat yourself up when those distractions come and you miss a beat, or several beats. Your people need to see you model that process and that level of authenticity, not just with others, but with yourself. OK, I'm done again. Forgive me?"

"Yes, honey, of course. As long as someone else agrees with you besides me!"

"Oh, Pastor, I think Donna is right on," said Mark. "My small group leaders regularly tell me the stories you tell on yourself are the most memorable and meaningful. Going even deeper will just inspire them to do the same. They know everyone is different and they know how to translate your examples into their own situation. I'm always surprised at how much depth our people are able to handle these days. It's really exciting to think that we are just scratching the surface!"

"Well, if I start going much below the surface, you all had better be ready! No telling what could happen. It's a bit scary, but I suppose, no, I know, you are right. I have to be willing, most of all, to be vulnerable. If I'm not willing to share my inner struggles publicly, that sets a bad example for others privately. Even more of concern to me is that many, especially the men, may not know that they need to be vulnerable, not just within their own family, but with themselves.

"We saw the benefits of moving in that direction with the men's retreat and the impact that new level of transparency had on the small groups. Mark and I even experienced it earlier with personal revelations during my first sabbatical. And then I had even more restoration at a weekend encounter that helped me see how my controlling spirit was unintentionally hurting my wife and family. Maybe I need to be more open about these experiences and look into making a similar program available to the church. It was so personal that I didn't even consider trying to push it on others. Maybe it's time to get over myself and help others look more deeply inward. It's definitely scary, but so worth it.

"Bottom line, I guess I've learned the hard way that we have to be intentional about asking the Holy Spirit to search out our own thoughts and anxieties. We have to be real and admit these things, ask forgiveness for our sins, whether intentional or unintentional, and then move on in Christ's strength. The same transparency and intensity we showed at our salvation we also need to show daily in our confessions. That's the only way we can remain holy, and by that, I mean retaining our special relationship with Christ, knowing that we can love ourselves as the Father loves us.

"You all have richly demonstrated that today. I am so proud of this group. But I am willing to humble myself by being open and real about the journey I am on, if it will help even one person.

"So does anyone else have another thought? Yes, George?"

"Well, I think we've uncovered quite a lot today, and we have a pretty good plan to keep this movement going. I really appreciate your commitment, Pastor, to being transparent in the pulpit, as you have been personally. I think that will speak volumes to our church body. I don't know what the future holds, but I know that I am looking forward to the new things that God will do in our midst.

"My only suggestion at this point is to widen the circle of feedback. By that I mean to get input and ideas from the people. I know we don't regularly do surveys, but maybe this is one time it would be appreciated and useful. I think it's part of being vulnerable. To allow others to speak, as you have done with this group today, and then really, really listen. Who knows, we might have some people God is actually speaking to and who have the next breakthrough idea for the Outpouring, or for the church body in general. Anyway, that's my thought. Take it for what it's worth."

"George, that's a great way to end this session. Would you mind taking the lead on drafting some survey questions and get a few others together, maybe one staff member and several others at random from the congregation to help you? You might also get ideas on the best way to conduct the survey. Let's start the process by listening. Personally, I'm not very good at that, especially when there are so many diverse voices. But I'm willing to be vulnerable, as you say, on this point. I'm going to hear a lot of ideas anyway, so we might as well give everyone the chance and see what themes come out of it."

"Sure, Pastor, I'd be happy to. And if anyone in this room wants to volunteer, see me after the session."

"Speaking of which, the end of the session, that is, I thank everyone for your time and thoughtful, prayerful input today. This has been very gratifying, especially receiving direct revelation through the Holy Spirit. We live in perilous times, and it is critical that we learn how to walk out these precious truths and continue to receive God's Outpouring, as a body and as individuals. We certainly went a lot deeper today than I was expecting. Just goes to show that I need to give the Holy Spirit even more freedom to work through others. I pledge to each of you to continue to ask, and then to listen. You have been a great encouragement to me today.

"And now may the Lord bless you and keep you in that secret place, under the shadow of His wings. And may He lift up His countenance upon you with joy and approval, and may He give you peace, the Shalom that satisfies your spirit, soul, and body with every good gift from heaven. Amen and amen."

# Epilogue

In my first book, *The Tower: A Parable of Relationships*, I told a simple story using unnamed characters to emphasize a number of teaching principles, primarily involving relationships. While many of the principles were based on Scripture, there was no explicit mention of God or theology. *The Organic Church: A Story of Revival*, in contrast, is very theological and deals with deep personal issues of one's relationship to God and others. The characters have names, personalities, and serious problems. However, the main purpose of the book is still to illustrate important principles that can help prepare the church, as Christ's Bride, for His soon coming. As a result, while this is in the form of a fictional story, it is not a traditional novel, but rather a series of teachings illustrated by the hopes, fears, trials and aspirations of a typical Spirit-filled pastor.

Writing a book like this would be a formidable task for an established author and pastor, but I am neither. I am a layperson who has been in the Spirit-filled culture since my salvation in 1975. I have been a deacon in a Baptist church and was a board member of a large Pentecostal church for twenty years, the founding pastor of which had to leave due to a moral failure. We have attended several other medium and large sized churches as a result of job moves. I have taught End Times classes, and my wife and I have taught adult Sunday school, and more recently classes in Restoring Relationships, a program developed by Christian psychologist Dominic Herbst. The principles of this program have had a huge impact on me and my family, and they are used liberally throughout *The Tower* and *The Organic Church*.

A key inspiration for this book is my third son, Ben, who is a pastor at a new work he helped launch in Pensacola, Florida. His commitment to his wife and three sons, his co-pastors, and his church members, is supernaturally anointed. He has lived and taught the Restoring Relationships principles and embodies the spirit of the organic church in so many ways. Ben, I love you and salute you.

My wife has held every position in large Christian K-12 schools, earned her doctorate, and is currently an adjunct professor at a Christian university. As you can imagine, I have seen the inner workings of large Christian ministries up close and personal. We recently downsized and moved to the central downtown area of Dallas where we are serving in a wonderful new urban church plant. I am still working as an IT project manager for a law firm and have felt led to write books on various topics.

I have a couple of engineering degrees, am an analyst, consultant, and science and End Times enthusiast. In these roles, I long ago established a principle of trying not to draw conclusions prematurely, but rather of gathering a lot of data and letting that data suggest patterns and conclusions. Especially in studying End Times, I discovered that we often are taught specific ideas which then become preconceived lenses through which we interpret additional information. So-called scientists do this all the time, especially those who don't believe in a God who sovereignly created everything for a purpose. The modern science community has spent hundreds of billions of dollars trying to understand the universe, and particularly its origins, in natural terms. As a result, they have concocted elaborate explanations and theories that cannot be proven and that have contributed to a society that is moving far away from Godly principles, preparing the way for the End Times judgments foreseen in the Bible.

The church, however, has often followed the same path of latching onto preconceived ideas that are not well founded on the Bible. That causes divisions and strife within the body of Christ. The body of Christ is meant to function in unity and harmony, so, as with science, there must be simple principles that we are unaware of, ignoring, or intentionally shutting out that prevent us from loving and trusting one another. This book has been a story about finding those principles and what can happen as a result. Writing it has been an intimidating but exhilarating experience in listening to the Holy Spirit, and writing as best I can the words and thoughts as they come. I hope you have found the results to be interesting, challenging, and inspirational. I hope even more that you will pray about which areas are most relevant to your personal situation, and that, like these characters, you will humble yourself before a mighty God who wants to mold you into an End Times warrior and saint. But that's another story…

11/7/19

Wow! There are no words to explain this Book to Some one. Because of Clay's Profession, I feel as if the Holy Spirit down loaded & wrote this. Clay just doesn't have the experience. I will read this again in late 2019/early 2020. There is so much more I can learn about the nature of God.

## About the Author

Clay Watts has worked in information technology for over forty-five years as a programmer, business analyst, manager, and process consultant. He has been a deacon, board member, and teacher in the areas of End Times and restoring relationships. His wife, Kathy, holds a doctorate in education and is an adjunct professor at a Christian university.

Clay and Kathy live in Dallas, Texas, and have four children and twelve grandchildren. They have served in various capacities at a number of large and small churches.

Made in the USA
San Bernardino, CA
02 June 2017